it was september when we ran away the first time

it was september when we ran away the first time

d. james smith

atheneum books for young readers: new york london toronto sydney

Atheneum Books for Young Readers * An imprint of Simon & Schuster Children's Publishing Division * 1230 Avenue of the Americas, New York, New York 10020 * This book is a work of fiction. Any references to historical events, real people, or real locales are used fictitiously. Other names, characters, places, and incidents are products of the author's imagination, and any resemblance to actual events or locales or persons, living or dead, is entirely coincidental. * Copyright © 2008 by D. James Smith * All rights reserved, including the right of reproduction in whole or in part in any form. * Book design by Michael McCartney * The text for this book is set in Bell MT. * Manufactured in the United States of America * FIRST EDITION 10 9 8 7 6 5 4 3 2 1 * Library of Congress Cataloging-in-Publication Data * Smith, D. James, 1955– * It was September when we ran away the first time / D. James Smith. —1st ed. * p. cm. * Summary: In Orange Grove, California, in 1951, plans for an upcoming carnival and running away part-time fall by the wayside when twelve-year-old Paolo, his six-year-old brother Georgie, and their ten-year-old deaf cousin Billy become victims of prejudice after Billy befriends a Chinese American girl. * ISBN-13: 978-1-4169-3809-5 * ISBN-10: 1-4169-3809-5 * [1. Race relations—Fiction. 2. Prejudices—Fiction. 3. Chinese Americans—Fiction. 4. Coming of age—Fiction. 5. Family life—California—Fiction. 6. Deaf—Fiction. 7. People with disabilities—Fiction. 8. California—History—1950—Fiction.] I. Title. * PZ7.S644645It 2008 * [Fic]—dc22 * 2008004819

for ernest and robin

acknowledgments

With special thanks to my editor, **jordan brown**, *for his talent and care; to my agent,* **barbara markowitz**.

1.

I'M UP EARLY THIS MORNING IN SEPTEMBER
of the year Billy got shamed, beat on, and worse, and ended up
having more need of running away than we ever dreamed when
we thought of it. You know, when you run away part-time, like
we did that first afternoon after class, go live in a tree house
four blocks out in the country from your own house and live
there after school every day and go home for meals and to sleep
and to read the paper, then no one actually knows you have run
away, it's the best way to do it.

Right then, it's just the first morning of school at John Muir Junior High and Billy won't get up. Billy's my cousin who is deaf. He's sleeping in my room in the same bed as my little brother, Georgie. Georgie is barely six years old and only about seven inches wide and a yard long so there's plenty of room in there for the both of them.

Georgie's hard to wake too, so I got to lift his eyelids, my thumbs and forefingers careful to clamp on his eyelashes, soft, like they're butterfly wings and then pull up on them, careful, *and* I have to do it without accidentally poking his eyes out, which is not my intention, though if it happened I would still be his brother and look out for him and get him some pencils or brooms to sell and most likely even train Rufus, our dog, to be his eyes. Georgie has nothing to worry about.

I have them open and the eyeballs in there are sagging limp all over the place like some of that Japanese sushi that's gone bad so I know he's still sleeping, and I blow on his eyeballs just this little bit to wake him, gentle and courteous. And he does wake up. Big brown eyes swelling up like bubbles rising to the surface of a deep, secretive lake, coming up and popping with terror. He sits up stock-still, and I leave off holding his eyelashes, pull back both my hands, lifting them, quick, quick, like a magician or the conductor of an orchestra just in time for his little-brother screaming to come blaring out of his mouth like the hard, sour blasts of a trumpet, "Waaa, waaaaa . . ."

Then he gets his mind around the fact that he's just being waked, doesn't like it but still calms down some 'cause he knows it's the first day of school, and I'm doing him a favor having promised I'd get him up in time to walk with me and Billy, and because I squish his mouth closed with my hand. He just sits there the way a little brother is supposed to, shoulders slumped until I let go, and then he rubs his eyes with his knuckles, relaxes, and starts yawning. Georgie isn't really afraid of me because he knows I'm his brother and God has me under commandment to love him, and it has always been our family's way to go along with the Bible or leastways on the interesting bits.

And even with Georgie's making like a trumpet, Billy just lies there under the covers, his legs all akimbo like he's been recently shot. And then I remember he's deaf. I forget it all the time, because Billy and I can sign and because we know each other well and have had so many adventures together ever since he came to live with our family this past summer that we can just about read each other's mind. Can do it almost as well as Margarita. She's the one of my sisters who's sixteen and an Italian beauty. Sometimes she'll put a red bandana on her head and some big bangly earrings and pretend she's Madam Sophie, who is a professional mind reader and prophet of the nonbiblical kind that lives in a one-bedroom house right next to the highway with a sign made out of little pink lightbulbs that blink and say, FORTUNES — $5, FORTUNES — $5, and so on and on.

Margarita can do fortune-telling pretty well. She once told me at three in the afternoon that I was going to get in trouble very soon, and by five thirty that evening my dad was after me about the snakeskin cowboy boots of his I was wearing. I knew more or less I wasn't supposed to mess with them, but he wasn't wearing them; he never wore them, 'cause they were showy and my dad is a studier of the part of scripture that says shun all that is worldly, which means no wearing Hawaiian shirts or gold chains or having a car that runs on a regular basis nor wearing those boots, even though they were a gift from my grandpa Leonardo and even if it would be kind of like walking around on Satan, who has been documented as having shown up occasionally as a snake. Probably my dad got disturbed 'cause I had to stuff four sets of his boxers, a shaving brush, and one of his ties down in there with my feet so those boots wouldn't come off.

Anyway, I did get in trouble exactly as Margarita had predicted, looking up at me from my palms she had in her soft hands, her big, kind rabbit eyes blinking as she's saying, "Paolo." (That's my given name, though sometimes when I'm talking to myself I call myself Ishmael, for no reason I know.) "Paolo," she says. "You should get those ridiculous boots off right this instant or Dad is going to kill you." I'm not a prophet of any kind, so how did I know she had real powers and that I should've minded her warning?

Plus, I knew my dad is usually distracted, doesn't notice much of what any of his kids are doing. He's got too many of them, I suppose. We're all mixed breed—a mother who is Italian and a dad who is Irish, by way of Tennessee and now, California. There are ten of us, plus Cousin Billy and my uncle Charlie, who lives in the attic, and also my mom, whom my dad does give attention on account she feeds him. He never learned how to cook and would starve if he didn't have my mom to look after his stomach. When Maria-Teresina-the-Little-Rose was born—she's my baby sister who is four—and my mom was in the hospital, dad made us water and peanut butter and jelly sandwiches, minus the jelly, for three days and nights. Mostly, my mom is the one managing our cases, and as well as any social worker or a probation officer ever could, Ernie says. He's my twenty-one-year-old brother who works full-time and is about to get married, and probably my best adviser.

Well, I guess Dad wasn't distracted enough on that particular day to miss noticing I was occupying his boots without permission, and he takes me up to his room and makes me sit on his bed. Shuts the door so my twin sisters Alice-Ann and Aurora can't make me any of their business, which is their favorite sport next to trapping our cat, Alfred, and squeezing him into these little outfits of a sailor or test pilot or whatever is their fancy they've sewn for him.

Dad begins, slow, like he always does when he gives you a "session." A session is when he sits in a little wooden chair he's got next to his nightstand while you sit on the bed. "Look at me when I'm talking to you," he always says. Parents say that, which is sort of ridiculous, because they know you can hear them plenty well and staring at a person isn't polite, and in a spot like that any sensible kid is on his best behavior and not going to be doing it.

Well, he's just looking at me and puckering his lips all sour with disappointment, his eyes soft but steady the way a tiger's eyes are half-lidded when it is counting up just exactly how it is going to gnaw on you. Like maybe thinking, I will swat this boy's head with one paw quick-like, or perhaps I'll jump on him and clutch his body with all four claws and pop his whole head in my mouth like a Tootsie Pop. Cats have blood cold as icebox water, Ernie says, and could enjoy playing a game of Ping-Pong with your head as much as eating it.

But I know my dad's not cold in his blood, 'cause he likes us all well enough to go work as a fireman on the Southern Pacific Railroad on a regular basis—he's gone days at a time—so we can have our house and the station wagon–full of groceries we eat four times a week. He just has a mind that goes wandering and sometimes will pat you on the head and say, "Good boy, Rufus," instead of your actual name.

So he's just watching me and I know I have to watch back, and then I know he is the real mind reader of the family, 'cause I can tell he's climbed in my head right through the windows of my eyes and is walking round opening closets and drawers and reading the homework I didn't finish and sitting around lounging on all the furniture and taking his time and trying the place out to see if it is set up in the way he thinks I should be living or not.

And that's it. He comes out, climbs back into his self, and his eyes go from tiger to dad eyes and he blinks and starts thinking about something else and just says, "You can have those boots when you are big enough to fit them if you are so inclined."

And, of course, his giving them to me like that makes me realize I was trespassing on his footwear and shouldn't do a thing such as that, and I just nod and look at them on the floor and go out of there quiet, but pulling the door open fast so that Aurora and Alice-Ann fall into the room with a *thud, thud* and jump up, faces red as bricks and smoothing their dresses and doing a little curtsy to my dad, then flying out of there like the little witches-in-training that they are.

Well, right now I'm not getting anywhere standing in my bedroom thinking—Billy can't read my mind, nor will he wake up just by me or Georgie making a racket. We got to get to school, so I take an athletic sock the color of coffee that is ripe from lying for six weeks in a pile of laundry in the corner of the room, and I wave it back and forth under Billy's nose the way a trainer will do to a boxer when he's sitting on his lonely little stool after the fourteenth round.

And Billy's head goes up slowly and his arms are swimming round all waterlogged, and he's making little awful mewling sounds like Alfred did once when my sisters outfitted him like George Washington with a little wig they'd made out of cotton balls and glued to his head. Then Billy nods back off to sleep, and I know I have to get him awake so we can get going—to school and running away after.

At that time, we didn't have any need for running away, really, excepting the sport of it; we were bored and wanted some fun and a place of our own. Plus we were at that difficult age when on account of our hormones and such we're confused and grown folks can't make sense of us. Leastways, that's what I was told in P.E. Health 2 the year before. Health 1 was about pimples and taking baths on a regular basis. Health 2 was mostly hormones, cells, tadpoles, and dental hygiene. Coach said girls have it even harder than guys and that's probably true, since I don't understand my sisters very well, excepting that if I cross one of them and she catches me, she'll sock my eyeballs loose while telling me I should straighten up and act a gentleman before it is too late. Now that I think on it, maybe we ran away just so's to have a little elbow room.

I wouldn't even have had the time to manage part-time running-away except I had quit my paper route just before school started. I never had wanted that paper route and only got it during the summer because Billy was mad for doing it. I never like saying no to Billy, because he is a rare one and true. Never would hurt you and always thoughtful about folks. Once he made me apologize to Mrs. Hanoian, one of our neighbors, for feeding some of her prize roses to Georgie. I read you could eat rose petals and not die. It was only two roses and she never missed them and Georgie thought it was nice, how I mixed them in with his tuna fish sandwich and all. But Billy made me apologize.

He's the kind that will pick up a whole caravan of snails when they've set out over the sidewalk for China or wherever and put them down carefully, right on the leaves of my mom's geraniums. Says with his hands, signing, *They got a right to a good lunch, same as us, Paolo.* He's like that natural, even though his dad died and his mom would as soon not have him around—the reason he's living with us.

We did that paper route for two weeks at the end of summer and made our collections, got the money, and then I was for quitting. Billy was reluctant at first, but then signed, *Paolo, keeping my life straight, and you and our customers happy, is making me feel my head is a bowling ball banging around in a dump truck.* So we agreed to let another kid have a chance at it. That's generous, that's Charity and a virtue, and, on account Billy and I are altar boys at the Cathedral of San Joaquin, we have to keep current on virtue.

Mostly virtue is a thing you don't plan. It just comes about of itself. Say, for instance, your sister Shawna, who is thirteen and a know-it-all person with freckles peppered all over her nose and cheeks and big hair frizzed out like Frankenstein's fiancée, was to have five dollars in change in a ceramic piggy bank she kept on her dresser. And say you were to have need of some little portion of those savings from time to time because you were runned-away, part-time.

And say that particular sister, Shawna, kept a watch on her stash. Well, you would have need of the virtue of Patience—and also a little cunning. And Courage. Shawna isn't any bigger than me, and she's not one to sock me either. She's got a fighting style all her own, some brand of wrestling. What that girl will do is clamp down on some part of you with her teeth, your wrist or your leg or your head, like a pit bull, and stay clamped until you are tired of not being able to go on with your life and give up and do whatever it is she wanted in the first place.

So there I still am in my room that morning, jingling one dollar ninety-five cents of courage in my pocket, thinking I *got* to get Billy awake, when I decide to place two quarters on his eyes as if he was fresh dead and laid on a table in the living room the way my great-granddad, who got himself smothered in a coal mine, was back in Tennessee when my dad was a kid.

His grandpa got smothered in a coal mine along with a Shetland pony they had down there to haul coal. They buried that pony right in the Baptist church cemetery and even trotted his horse-folks out there for the funeral. Ernie says those ponies never cried. Said ponies won't cry, but they'll buck their heads, sorrowful, turn away and stare out into a field—then, when you're not looking, kick you hard out of discouragement, on account they don't get paid for coal mining the way they should.

Finally, Billy's mouth starts mumbling and his hand goes up to scratch his eyes and knocks those quarters off, and then he yawns and sits up and sees me. Georgie watches where those quarters go rolling on the worn hardwood floor and dives after them, quick.

I smile at Billy.

He smiles with half of his face and squints one eye down at me, then gives me a little wave with his hand.

I say, "It's today now, so get up and let's go."

2.

Billy shakes the sleep from his head,
stretches once, and rolls out of bed. He can read lips pretty
good. Learned it on his own first, then got taught, formal, by
Mrs. Hanoian in her kitchen every day in the afternoon. Mrs.
Hanoian had a brother who was deaf, and also, she knows all
kinds of stuff they teach in college like, "I think, therefore I am."
That's philosophy. Means you're alive. College is chock-full of
stuff like that. Imagine if you just thought you were dead your
whole life. And imagine you didn't even know it.

We'd already learned signing from books at the public library and from Hector, my second oldest brother and the brain of the family—he's eighteen—and from Shawna, my one-year-older-than-me, wrestling sister.

We let Mrs. Hanoian think she taught us, since we don't think she has any reason for living except us and her roses and a parakeet named Bob. And her red and white Ford V8 convertible and her boyfriends, Albert the plumber and Nazdah Azoyan, who owns a thousand acres of raisins and takes her to Hawaii and Paris or London every year.

Well, Billy and Georgie get dressed in a flash, and we three zip downstairs to get some coffee. Our family is big, so my mom has a cafeteria coffeepot going all the time and you don't have to wait for everybody to eat breakfast. My folks think it is nonsense that coffee makes you short. Being half-Italian is what does it. You could just look at my mom or my grandma and grandpa Leonardo and know that. If Grandpa didn't have a bald head and gold teeth and wear his trousers up high around his big middle you would think he was in third grade. Once I saw him and Grandma Leonardo go by in their Buick, and I knew it was them only 'cause I recognized the shine on the top of my grandpa's head and my grandma's hair that she keeps rolled up on top of hers. It was that bun I saw and so knew for sure it was them. I waved, though their eyes were not high enough to see out the window at me.

Anyway we're allowed to make breakfast ourselves if we don't burn up the kitchen like my mom did once when she was cooking fried chicken and talking to Mrs. Beyer, our next-door neighbor, and changing diapers and vacuuming the dining room, all at the same time. My mom is a saint, is what Margarita says. Taking care of our whole tribe and doing the Ladies Altar Society on Wednesdays and thinking about God while she's washing windows near hard enough to break them, hissing in English-Italian, "Jesu, Marie, a-Lordy sakes alive."

In the kitchen it's only me and Billy and Georgie and my sister Betsy, who is seventeen and goes to business college instead of high school because she prefers typing to philosophy and figures that Mr. Willard, the manager at Pacific Telephone, who says he will make her his secretary when she's done with typing lessons, already knows he is alive and thinking and wouldn't need her telling him college philosophy. He's thinking about Betsy's big blue eyes and maybe marrying her too, Ernie says.

She says, "You guys want some eggs? I'll make you some if you like." Betsy is a big dieter and wants to make us stuff whenever possible so she can nibble half of it before it gets to the table. That way she can stay on her diet. But this is our big day and we are too nervous to eat more than six or seven pieces of toast each. We make those ourselves in the toaster. We scoot down and scrunch up at the other end of the table from Betsy when she sits down to eye our munching.

When we hear people which we know are our family start to clunk down the stairs, we fly out of there so's we don't have to sit down and eat properly, which means waiting for my dad to finish his meal before we can leave the table. My dad believes it builds character to watch him chew his food, putting his silverware down between bites and dabbing his mouth with the big bib he wears tucked into his collar.

He's got lots of character. He fixed up our house, working on it all his life when he was home from riding on the back of the train. Our house could be a rich person's house, because it has a big porch with columns and a balcony on top of it and an attic for a third story. In fact, back in 1919, the mayor of Orange Grove City lived there. He added the attic later when he met a French businesswoman that he took a fancy to, and so had to have a special room built for his wife. Ernie says look close and you can see scratches she made on the walls up there. I have and don't see them, but I know it's mostly ignorant not to trust my brother, 'cause he has made it all the way to the time to move out on his own. He's getting married to Amber Anosini, says he's just waiting to save enough for a place with an extra room up top. Just in case.

3.

I watch Georgie skipping ahead on the sidewalk and smile. The best part of going back to school is that it happens in September and gives us time to get planning for October, when over at our church they have the big Irish and Italian All Saints' Day/Mexican Day of the Dead/Chinese Lantern Night, or as Ernie calls it: American Halloween. He's right, 'cause we do some trick or treating as well as running around at that carnival. He's right, also, because our church has all kind of folks that go to it, and from what I understand,

Monsignor adds another part to the carnival every couple of years so that all will come and feel welcomed and satisfied with Halloween and Catholicism.

Catholicism is smart that way. If you're Catholic and want to start up a new branch of Catholic, say you're a monk and unhappy with the color of your robes, you get six or seven other guys together and write a letter to the pope, and he'll usually let you start your own group and wear any kind of robe you want—as long as you don't get too colorful. That's how Catholics keep up their numbers and don't have folks starting all kind of new religions, which there may be enough of anyway.

Ernie says I could grow up and be a priest myself if I can't think of anything else to do with my life. Says I'd get to wear all kinds of fancy getups like Alfred the cat and live in a house with a cook, and if I got promoted to Monsignor I'd have a '47 Ford with mashed bumpers to drive and Mike Callahan on his Harley-Davidson as a police escort when I'm coming home from Murphey's Place every night, where I'd also have a tab that I don't ever have to pay. Says I could do worse, and keep it in mind.

I know Georgie's mind is more on school than careers or even the carnival. That's 'cause he's going to Yosemite Elementary, first grade. He's already done time there for kindergarten and knows the layout, but still he's excited. He's bouncing along the sidewalk ahead of me and Billy. "Hurry up, you guys," he keeps saying.

Billy is ten now and in fifth grade. Mr. Gladstone, the editor of the newspaper, is the school board president and is our friend on account we got to know him when we were paper boys this past summer. He took a special interest in Billy then, when he found out he had trouble hearing. Tried to get Billy interested in being a jet pilot or whatever he wanted to be. Anyway, Billy is going to get to go to school in Orange Grove this fall.

Hector says some of the teachers didn't think it was such a hot idea. Maybe they haven't had many deaf kids in school around here, but in a little town the school board calls all the shots they care to, and those teachers have instructions to just let Billy come to class and do the best he can. They even got to hire Mrs. Hanoian's niece, who can sign just as good as Mrs. Hanoian, to help Billy and go to his classes with him two days a week. Hector says that's a first for the school, and a good one.

I know Billy went to school somewheres when he lived with his mom in Tarzana. But when he came back from this last visit, he said she was taking another long trip with her boyfriend and so he's got to stay with us this fall, same as he did all summer. We're glad to have him. I know Billy misses his dad ever since he passed on, but I don't think he misses his mom all that keen since she took up with the plumber she's so fond of.

His and Georgie's school is right next to mine. We get there and those two go in and there's a slew of kids all over the yard, and Georgie turns and give me a last little wave and shouts, "Bye, Paolo, bye, Paolo," some pleading there in his voice as if suddenly he realizes maybe he's a little like a fellow going off to be hanged.

Their school is all one story and looks the way those science stations they have down in Antarctica do, built out of something that looks like plywood and Styrofoam, like it was thrown up fast and cheap, which is what is known as modern.

I'm in seventh grade for the second time, due to the fact I skipped kindergarten and started early and then didn't do so well last year, so they are making me do seventh all over. I know I learned everything I needed but just never quite got around to writing it up when they gave tests and such. I don't mind since I was the shortest kid in my class last year, and this way I will be the shortest kid in a class of people my own age.

My school has two stories and big columns at the front steps like the Supreme Court. Ernie and Hector told me architecture is a science and an art, and the going-in places, the entries of buildings, are designed to make you feel little and humble and on your best behavior. They said notice how the richer a person is the grander the going-in part of their house is. Said the very richest don't even have any company on account of this, and that's how they have time for golfing and Republicanism and keeping track of the prices of barrels of oil, which are all things they are keen on.

Anyhow, in the fall, all day at school when you are bored with your lessons, you can think about the church carnival and what you will do to help out. Billy already signed himself up for all kinds of stuff. Baseball pitching booth helper, BB-gun shooting gallery helper, hot dog and Coke helper, and so on. Even though we go to public school, most everybody around here still goes to the Halloween carnival, whether they are part of our church or not, so even some of the teachers remind us to think about what we are going to sign up for.

Myself, I am trying to think of a brand-new booth we could design of our own and run and make so much money doing it we could keep a little for ourselves and no one would mind or even know—the way Ernie told me the Italians who run Las Vegas do.

I was thinking about that when Mrs. Ogilbee, my period one pre-algebra teacher, calls on me and puts the blush on me complete, saying, "Is a certain person under the impression that summer vacation isn't over?" Says that while she's standing next to my desk with her hand like a bat that's just dropped on my shoulder. I'm that certain someone. She's said that on account everyone but me has a pencil and a blank piece of paper out on their desks. I usually have paper out to make little drawings and write letters using the French military code that Hector taught to me and Billy. I don't usually write pre-algebra notes, because I know there are already plenty of atom bombs in the world and doubt I could find any other work where I'd need math that is half numbers and half squiggles and angles. I don't think it is on account I am lazy or that I don't understand all this two to the power of three stuff and such, but I think I would be satisfied my whole life just watching atom bombs and algebra. We get to see that over my grandpa's house, since he has a television and tunes in whenever Las Vegas is blowing up some of its desert. Hector thinks the Italians made a deal with the government to do the bombs there so as to keep the tourists happy when they are too tired from gambling.

Now that it is 1951, we have to have an Atomic Energy Commission to keep track of bombs and the Russians. We don't want them thinking North America would be a good place to come live and set up Communism. I am not 100 percent sure on what Communism is, except it is especially bad and would cause everyone to have bad dental hygiene and drink so much vodka they'd want to dance whilst squatting.

I get a piece of fresh paper and my pencil out and try to concentrate on what Mrs. Ogilbee is saying now about pre-algebra, but her hand on my shoulder is all I can think about, even though I know the next question she asks will be coming my way. "So . . . what would be the product of eleven times three?" she says.

Of course, nobody answers except for Corky Diller, who is the tallest girl in our entire school and is, right now, half killing herself squirming in her desk and waving her hand to be called on as usual. Pretty much everybody hates her when she does that, but no one beats her up or anything, because she's pretty and too big and squirmy and maybe 'cause she takes the heat off the rest of us with her answering questions all the time. I start feeling little bat-bites on my shoulder and know that is encouragement to not be bashful and go on and say what the answer is. I close my eyes like I am putting some serious thought on things and twist my pencil around in my hand. Push out my lips like I am almost onto it and then like, *whoosh*, it got away from me, so I have to shake my head with sorrow at its going.

I look up at Mrs. Ogilbee and don't blink so some tears will come up in my eyes, just a little, which is a last-ditch effort and can't be used all the time, but it is only day one of school and I'm not up to speed and I have to. Mrs. Ogilbee sees those tears swelling up and goes soft and plucks her hand off me and moves down the row and taps Hiram Sarkisian on the back of his head very lightly. Hiram knows answers but doesn't like to give them. He is Armenian, and his dad told him that you shouldn't do work unless you get wages, and I know by Hiram's way of thinking there isn't any profit in school. But he answers, polite like his family wants him to be. "Thirty-three," is all he says. I'm glad I know somebody in the seventh grade, second time around.

And Mrs. Ogilbee goes on with her lecture, and I know she won't bother me anymore, which gives me time to think about the Atomic Energy Commission and watching Communists and the carnival and all manner of things. I put things together and get it down on the coded message I will give to Billy through the chain-link fence at lunchtime. Billy doesn't see any reason for me to write in code, since we could talk in sign language if we wanted to and nobody at school but Mrs. Hanoian's niece knows signing, but I think it gives life a bit of zing to do things nobody understands. Don't you?

So I write in code, *Why don't we keep folks in Orange Grove under surveillance between now and the end of October? Instead of working at other booths at the carnival, we could have our own with Margarita telling fortunes. By then we'd know all manner of things about people, could sit under Margarita's table and whisper stuff up to her!*

4.

HECTOR TOLD ME THERE WERE TWO KINDS of Communists. Russian Communists and Chinese. Both are called Reds. It's the Red Chinese that interest me. There are five hundred million of them. They live packed tight and are used to it. Say you lived in Shanghai in a one-bedroom apartment, you could live there with your entire family, all your aunts and uncles and cousins in bunk beds, six or eight high, and not feel squeezed. They cook on a little stove on their balconies, and most every single person has a bicycle of their own. Mao Tse-tung, their president, gave them all bicycles and lots of instructions on how to be a Red and not care if you don't have automobiles.

Hector told me that there are so many of them that if it doesn't rain like it's supposed to and the crops don't grow as they should, they have to make bread out of dirt. I don't know how that would work, but Communists are cunning. I wouldn't have believed him, except he showed me about it from his Peoples of the World encyclopedia that he got at a yard sale for a down payment of a nickel and the promise to cut Mrs. Sweeney's lawn come summer. We know Mrs. Sweeney from church. She used to be a school librarian and probably hauled more than a few books home in her day, 'cause she's always got plenty to spare for her yard sales.

The Red Chinese don't drink vodka or have any special dances I know of. They got Communism, because it is sort of like a disease and spreads easy if you live in a place without proper plumbing and regular meals. Ernie says we won't ever get it here in America 'cause J. Edgar Hoover and the FBI won't have it. They keep tabs on anyone who even thinks Communism and that even some say the rest of us should do the same. Ernie says that when Mr. Fields, the high school shop teacher, and Mr. Koski, the biology teacher, started having Sierra Club meetings to keep the redwoods from being cut down, Mrs. Sweeney called the FBI on them and they disappeared for two weeks and came back and never had another redwood tree meeting.

Hector said that was on account they went deer hunting, and those meetings were for getting drunk and making lists of widows and married women they thought were still good-looking. That made some sense to me, since I'd never heard nothing but mostly good about those two. Hector and Ernie told me so much about Communism I could write a book on it, except I already own a book and don't see the need of another, whether it was one I wrote or not. Some of what I could write would even be true.

Anyway, when I come out of school, day one of my stretch, I'm curious to know what Billy thinks of my plan for the carnival. He wasn't at the chain-link fence at lunch, but Georgie was, and I gave him the note to pass on to Billy. I see Georgie right away running my way down the sidewalk. He's got a finger painting of some kind the size of a kite and his face is flushed-up, excited. He's got Rufus with him. Rufus walks the five blocks to school with us every day and knows to come get us when school lets out.

Rufus is our big St. Bernard and English sheepdog who is short on brains and big on friendly. Sometimes I get the feeling he is really, really smart and goes ignorant when it suits him. He's got a lazy streak, I know. He gets all the food and company he wants and without doing a lick of work, and that is something to be admired and possibly a thing I should study. Anyway, he can find his way around Orange Grove just fine. Right now, he's trotting along like a baby elephant behind Georgie, who shouts, "Paolo!"

I look around like I don't know him, like, who is that weird little kid, where is his keeper? It's not that I am ashamed of my family; it is that Corky Diller is walking behind me with her seventy-three girlfriends, and I know they are talking about me. Either they think I am cute or that I am kin to possum. Girls are like that. They will act like you're nothing around their friends, and then phone you up and ask after your day. I've had all the adventure I want with girls and don't plan on marrying until after I've been to Alaska, which I'm going to do when I turn eighteen. And Corky isn't Italian, and I've already promised my grandpa Leonardo I'd pick an Italian woman. He says Italians are the best for marrying, since they'll give you the best years of their lives and remind you of it on a regular basis whilst spatulas and frying pans are flying in your direction. He says those hot tempers of theirs keep them young, that ten seconds after they are done being mad, they will kiss you till you need emergency medical treatment.

Georgie doesn't know about women and just makes a beeline to me. "Paolo," he says, "I got to sit in the front row. Paolo, we made paintings. Miss Farisi put up a picture called *Starry Night* and we all copied it." He shoves the mess he made out of some poster paper at me. "Paolo, they gave us graham crackers and milk and didn't charge."

I take his picture and hold it at arm's length. It looks like somebody had painted Rufus purple and let him loose to roll on some paper. "Hmm . . . ," I say. "You may have real talent, Georgie."

"I know," he says softly. "Miss Farisi told me." He's already in love with her, I can tell, which makes sense since any guy in Orange Grove who isn't married is in love with her too, and even though she's a Miss and not a Mrs., she's probably on Mr. Koski's list. Since she is Italian, I was kind of thinking she'd be the first I looked up soon as I was back from Alaska.

I say, "You know, the guy who painted this picture cut his ear off?"

"I have both my ears, Paolo." Georgie has his head cocked sideways like a German shepherd.

"I mean the guy who did the original picture you all copied."

"Why'd he do that?"

"He was in love with a woman who didn't love him back."

"Did he look better after?"

"What?"

"Was his ear too big?"

"Georgie," I start to say, and then I see Billy, and for the first time in my life my brain won't make any words for my mouth to say.

"Paolo?" Georgie says from a long way off. "Paolo?"

Billy is crossing the street away from us and is holding out his arms like a cop stopping traffic because he is making especially sure no one runs over a little dark-haired Chinese girl wearing a red silk jacket with a black dragon sewn on it, curling up from her waist to her chin.

5.

"GET DOWN OFF THAT LADDER, GEORGIE!"

"I don't have to do what you say." Georgie keeps climbing, his face all squinched with concentration and concern for his safety.

I bump the ladder a little with the toe of my Converse high-tops from where I am in the tree house looking down on him. "You are six and have to do what I tell you."

"Not since you ran away I don't. I checked."

"Checked what?"

"I asked Shawna, and she said if you have run off, you don't have rights to me or any O'Neil."

"That's crazy, Georgie."

"I checked." He keeps coming and I step out of his way, since his head is coming up anyway, already knee-high to me. I just go on and grab his shoulders and haul him in like a dead shark onto a boat deck. Right or wrong, if he fell out of the tree, I'd get in trouble. I'm pretty sure the law would say his being my brother canceled out that I was runned-away, part-time, and since I'm not getting paid for running away, how would I even prove it without receipts?

Georgie goes on lying there and just swiveling his head round, checking out the tree house. It's an amazing place. It's twenty-five feet in the air and big as a wrestling ring with walls that go up to my waist all round. It's anchored to the tree, a hundred-year-or-probably-more-old oak, with big lag bolts and wires that run up to the high branches to support some of the weight and to stabilize it.

Like I said, the walls go up just halfway, so it has no roof and no need of windows. The deck is even with the first big fork in the tree, so those two trunks split off sideways right in the middle of it. It's got a hole cut in one corner of the floor with a fireman's pole to slide down if you care to and some little wooden steps going up one of the trunks to the next big branch if you'd like to go sit up there. It's level and foursquare and wouldn't come down in a hurricane. It wasn't kid-built.

Mr. Shalenbarger built it for his boys back before the war, World War II, before his two boys got drowned when their Victory ship went down on its way to England. They used to live in our house before we got it. Back then Mr. Shalenbarger owned the land out behind our place and used this bit of it for a place for his family to play when they weren't picking the pecans that grow there. I think those boys joined the navy 'cause the tree house with all its rigging and its sure deck and its swaying in hard weather makes you think you are sailing, sometimes.

Georgie has disturbed me and Billy; we are doing our runned-away stuff. I got Billy tied by his wrists to a branch over his head and since I am John Wayne this time, and a government man, I am doing the interrogating. Billy is a Russian radio operator I blew out of an attic in Berlin with a little brick of plastic explosives. Communist spies use short-wave radios all the time to report back to the Soviet Union all that's going on. Any time you see a person with a ham radio, you *know* you are most likely looking at some kind of spy. Normal folks use the telephone if they got something to say.

I just got through explaining to this radio-operating spy how John Wayne and Democracy was going to kick Joe

Stalin's rear and force the Communists to be free to do what they wanted except bother everybody and that he'd better tell me what exactly his mission is, what he's transmitting back to Russia.

It occurs to me that Georgie showing up just then was okay, since Billy talks with his hands, and I've got them tied and that's why Billy's been looking at me, dark, like I was a fool the whole time I was doing my speech and asking questions. Of course, I was going to actually quiz him about his Chinese girl-friend, if that's what she is. He walked her home today. And I know she's Chinese 'cause she is part of the Cheng clan, named Veronica, I think. The twins Matthew and Mark Cheng are in my grade and I've known her other brothers, John and Luke, too, since always. They go to our church, which is brave since most round here still haven't warmed up to Chinese persons.

I don't know why that is, since Orange Grove has every type of people. Maybe it is on account of the Red Chinese brand of Communism or 'cause they look something like the Japanese the USA had to fight in World War II. What I do know is that they sit in their very own pew in the back, and some in the Ladies Altar Society do a fair bit of whispering whenever their family comes to church, which they do regular and on time.

I want to know if she's Billy's girlfriend now and what's up with that? No ten-year-old boy should be interested in a girl, and certainly not a Chinese girl who wears red all the time.

"Can I get tied up?" Georgie asks. He's still lying there with his neck pretzeled, looking up at me.

"I don't know, Georgie," I say. "We already started with this and there is no way John Wayne would allow some squirt to get himself written into his movie after they'd started."

"You aren't John Wayne."

I don't answer 'cause the Duke wouldn't say anything to such as that. I hike up one side of my jeans and slump one shoulder. I look over at Billy and throw my arm off in Georgie's direction the way John would. "You know this spy?"

Billy just closes his eyes. He can't talk with his hands tied and he doesn't want to encourage me, knows I could go on like this for half an hour if I cared to.

"Tell you what," I say to Georgie. "Ya give me those quarters you snatched off the floor this morning, and I'll tie your hands and your feet, and blindfold you too, if that'll make you happy."

Georgie pulls those quarters out of his jeans pocket, quick, and stands up and hands them to me. I go to Billy and untie him and lash Georgie up lickety-split. I blindfold him with one of my sisters' bandanas and when he starts to tell me I got him tied too tight, stuff a sock in his mouth and leave him be. Billy is rubbing his wrists. We roll Georgie off into a corner where he goes on flopping like the fish slapped out on a dock that he is, and we go sit down, cross-legged on the floor. I figure I will ease into my curiosity so as not to spook Billy. "So you give any thought to my psychic booth idea for the carnival?"

Billy shakes his head.

"Well, you got any better ideas?"

He signs, *Margarita won't do it. Cheat like that.*

Right off I realize he's right. Margarita takes church to heart in an especial way. Probably 'cause she is an Italian beauty and has boys following her like she's dropping sugar cubes on the sidewalk wherever she goes. She knows she's got to be churchy to keep from getting in trouble, I suppose. "We could get Shawna to do it." Shawna is smart and when not in a mind to wrestle is mostly good to me and Billy, and she's saving her babysitting money to go to law school, so she'd see that our giving her answers from under the table wouldn't be cheating; she'd understand that it was just good presentation. Ernie says presentation is like drama, looking like you are a somebody or a something instead of actually being it. Like saying you're sorry to your sister for pulling her hair—which I only had to do to get her chompers out of my ankle—in front of your folks and hanging your head so the tears you force out will drip on your shoes. That's presentation.

Maybe, Billy signs. His lips are pushed out, thoughtful, like a chimpanzee's so I know he means it.

"Say, you ever know anyone had a china-doll girlfriend at Yosemite Elementary?" I say, offhand and bored-like.

Billy was facing me, but now he's looking hard over at Georgie.

"'Cause you know the Red Chinese are trying to get as much information as they can on how to build atom bombs."

Georgie is thrashing back and forth, his face like it's shucking the last of its fish-light.

"If the Russians won't give them the algebra they need to do it, they will have to get it from Americans."

Billy shoots up like a rocket and darts to Georgie. He yanks the sock out of his mouth and unties the blindfold and I see, then, Georgie's face is as purple as the drawing he'd made today at school. He sucks in a gallon of air to the fifth power and then sends it back out as a scream that says, "I'M TELLING!"

We got to calm him down, give him the quarters back, promise to let him be Humphrey Bogart next time. He thinks he could do a better Bogart than the Duke on account of his size. The worst is we have to promise him he can help us get all the FBI info on folks we think will be going to the carnival. And that's bunk. To the tenth.

6.

"Shhhhh . . ."

I have my hand tight over Georgie's mouth, but he's still making little gurgling noises. I leave his nostrils open so he doesn't turn into *Starry Night* again and blackmail us, this time, into being allowed to run away part-time with us too, or something. It got dark and once we got home, we all just finished our supper and went right up to bed and right out the second-story window of our room to the tree branches on the side of the house to the top of the wooden fence and down more into the driveway and then three houses over to Mrs. Sweeney's. We are snuck up to her living room window, that yellow light seeping out and our faces dark as raisins.

I have Uncle Charlie's binoculars he brought back from the Philippines, and Billy has a little notepad and a pencil. Georgie has himself and Rufus. Mrs. Sweeney is the most superstitious person we know on account she thinks her ancestors feel cozier as ashes clamped into little bronze canisters she keeps in a glass bookcase. Told us once that it was much more comforting to them than being out in the Belmont Avenue cemetery day and night, rain and fog in the winters, desert-hot in summers, and we are sure she will be a customer at the carnival. Now we just need some FBI-type info on her so we can tell her a good future.

So far all she's done is watched some TV and had some Jell-O she ate out of a green glass dish she put on a TV tray with wobbly legs that look like antennas. We don't have TV, so we are watching her show too, though we don't know what they are saying. It's too far away for Billy to read the lips of their talking.

We are just about to go on our way when Mr. Koski walks into the room wearing slippers, a long kitchen match just then flaring to light his pipe and his face. I drop my hand from Georgie's mouth since he's gone quiet too. Billy looks at me and shakes his head like, *Man, oh, man.* After all, Mrs. Sweeney was the one who was supposed to have turned him in for his Commie redwood forest meetings, and here she is having one with him all by herself.

I know that women in the middle of their ages get crazy because Ernie has explained it to me, but I never saw it directly. He says they will be sweet as pie one minute and go straight to slamming doors and barking like a dog the next. The only way to handle them then is to say, "Yes, dear," and back away slowly. They will snap out of it after they've had an hour or so to cry and fan themselves and have something cool to drink.

Billy flips open his notepad and scribbles quickly for a moment. Then we duck down and start to back off when Georgie says, "I didn't get to do my part."

"Your part is to hush and do what we say."

"No, it's not."

Billy makes slashing motions to his throat at the both of us.

"Yes, it is," I whisper.

"No. My part is to take pictures."

"Oh, you don't say," I say. Georgie has been known to tell a lie or two in his day. "If you are a photographer, then I am a giraffe," I say.

"You look like Paolo."

"Oh, please . . ."

"Shhhh," Georgie says to me then, putting one finger to his lips. Then he pulls out from under his sweatshirt a Brownie box camera that I know is my dad's.

"Georgie, give that to me this instant. Dad'll skin us and tack us up to dry if we break it."

"No, he won't."

"Oh, yeah, what makes you think that?"

"You know why. It's your camera. I got it out of your drawer under the T-shirts."

It's too dark for anyone to see me turn red, but I feel it, my head swelling up like a balloon of hot water.

"Give that to me," I hiss.

Just then Billy pokes my shoulder. I turn and see that Mr. Koski is standing at the front window and looking out into the blackness, in what seems to be right in our direction.

We all race out of there, spooked to our toes. We keep running until we get two blocks down, all the way to Van Ness where the California Hotel is and the parking lot lights and the streetlights there that are columns with big bulbs on top, sort of like giant candles planted in the park strips. We stop and lean over with our hands on our thighs and catch our breath. "Mr. Koski . . . is a . . . biologist . . . and . . . a Communist . . . no telling what might . . . have . . . happened to . . . us," I pant.

Billy shakes his head at me. He thinks I enjoy scaring myself, but there is no denying the truth of what I've said. I know it is absolutely faithful to what I've seen and imagined. We sit down there in a pool of lamplight and lie back on the grass. Billy rolls over and puts his hands above my face so I can see him sign, *We did get one good bit for fortune-telling.*

"Yeah, that is true," I say, perking up considerably.

Then I hear somebody shout, "That's them!" I sit up fast and look around to see nothing 'cause we're in a pool of light and outside of it the world is a dark cave. "We know what you're doing!" I hear that, then a *crack* like somebody getting a hit off a fastball and I jump up. Georgie jumps up too. Rufus lets out one halfhearted bark and gets up also, though in slow motion. But Billy doesn't. He's sitting there with a glazed look in his eyes like he doesn't know anything and never did, like his eyes aren't getting any reception nor giving up any info to his brain, and his mouth is sagged open with wet spiders of blood dangling down from his lips.

7.

GEORGIE'S ASLEEP IN THE CORNER NEXT TO
the fireman pole in our tree house. I'm examining Billy's teeth
with the four-battery chrome police flashlight I got for selling
one subscription of the *Grove County Guide* last summer. You
have to get folks to sign up for the paper if you have a paper
route, and that's one of the reasons I quit. I couldn't talk anyone into signing up, no matter that I told them if they did sign
I'd get to go to Harvard and my little brother would get the
wheelchair he's been wanting. So I signed my dad up, and

we've been getting the paper for half a month now. I got to figure a way to pay for it, since my dad's under the impression he gets one month free since I was wired in with the *Guide*.

The tooth that is to the left of his left eyetooth is wobbly when I test it. Billy slaps my face automatically when I do that, then signs, *Sorry.* He's the one asked me to check his chompers. His lip is split too, but not bad enough we think it needs doctoring. It was a rock that did it. A rock someone threw. A little round river rock, smooth and gray as a pigeon's egg. I know since we found that rock on the park strip and have it now. Have plans to throw it back at them that did this, whoever they are, first chance we get. Since Billy couldn't hear it I've explained what was shouted before that rock was thrown.

"That one is going to turn black and eventually fall out," I say. I have the flashlight to my face so he can read the lips of what I am saying.

Then I put the flash on him to see what he signs. He just nods and covers his eyes from the glare.

"A dead tooth isn't going to look very inviting to a certain little Chinese girl." I say that and then shoot the light back to Billy quick to see his reaction.

He glares at me, then thinks, then motions, *Okay. Pull.*

I puzzle on this a minute. The Duke would probably heat up a knife and give Billy a fifth of whiskey to drink, and then once he was out of his mind and singing, "Look away, look away, look away, Dixieland," he'd start carving. But this isn't a bullet in Billy's shoulder, and I swore years back not to touch liquor and besides, we aren't in high school and don't have vodka or rye whiskey or Bowie knives or anything even near that sort of thing.

"Give me your hands," I say to Billy, my face lit up again. It occurs to me if anyone was looking out toward that orchard they'd be wondering what's up with the little cone of light that is swinging round like a lighthouse, stabbing the darkness way out there up in a tree.

Is that really necessary? Billy signs.

"Absolutely," I say. I know darn well John Wayne would do something exactly like it. So I string Billy's wrists up over his head and take some fishing line I keep in a knothole up there along with a whole slew of stuff, and I tie it around Billy's tooth. That tooth is crowded in there with its brothers and it takes a bit to get just the one lassoed. I count out four yards of line and tie a brick we keep in the tree house to that end. Then I toss it overboard.

Billy can't talk, but he can make a pretty good *Waggaha-haaaaaa!* in a very interesting strangulating manner. I put the light on him while his mouth is open with that grunting, and sure enough that tooth is missing, and it doesn't seem bad to me at all, except for the look of it—black, bloody mess that it is. I tell Billy that but give him a minute to calm down and do some spitting before I untie him.

Georgie doesn't wake up but starts mumbling in his sleep. "No, Your Honor. No sir, never again. Paolo made me do it. Yes sir, I have the evidence right here."

I think he's been over my grandma's watching too much bad TV or something. I know it is time we got him and ourselves back to our house and our room and our beds. We've been runned-away from home long enough for one day. Billy goes slack some and I untie him. We sit down. "Who you think has it in for us?" I ask.

Billy is rubbing his cheekbone gently when he lifts his shoulders. *I don't know.*

I believe him, too, 'cause Billy keeps to himself and is polite to everyone should they ever bother to talk to him, give him a chance to be friendly, which mostly they don't on account of his deafness. And I know now that he has his special girl-friend, folks will be stepping especially careful round him. Even today at school when he was helping his girl across the street, well, Corky Diller and the seventy-three saw that and stopped walking and started circling each other, stepping round like a bunch of bees had been blown up their skirts. 'Course, they wouldn't say nothing directly.

Heck, even without all that, most already act like Billy's deafness is catching or they just can't be bothered, or they think since he doesn't talk, then he's stupid. All not true. Anyway, kids usually just ignore him. I don't know a time anyone's done something to him, direct, like this.

"You think Georgie did something?"

Billy shakes his head.

"Well, maybe whoever done it mistook our identities for some others."

I point the flash again at Billy. *No, there was lots of light there with the streetlamp and the parking lot lights. And Paolo, they said, "That's them."*

Yeah, I know that, I think to myself. I know. What would the Duke do now? Probably get mad and go sock someone, but who is there to sock? In the movies, socking somebody pretty much will take care of any problem you have. But I got a feeling it just ain't that simple. You'd think the government would have figured out some other way since the president and the premier of Russia are way older than me, yet it still seems they are set on having as many atom bombs as they can get, which if they use them would be the hardest socking of someone you could imagine. I guess the USA hasn't got a choice on account you can't trust a Communist, but atomic socking is worrisome to me, seems somebody smarter than me should put thought on it.

But right now, I'm mostly worried about Billy, and I think about surveillance and how we've only been playing J. Edgar Hoover, how if we want to find out who did this, then it's gonna be for real.

8.

"J. EDGAR WOULD NOT ALLOW ANY OF HIS government men, his G men, to date a Chinese girl unless she were under surveillance, but I see no reason to do FBI on Veronica," I say to Billy.

Billy just looks at me. I got the feeling he thinks all my Communist stuff is just acting a fool, and I think I know his girl ain't likely to be a real Red Chinese, though it's still an interest to me.

As for getting info on her for the carnival, a Chinese person knows way more about telling their own futures with tea leaves and coins they throw and wouldn't pay any dime to talk to my sister with a towel on her head or lipstick on or even six earrings in one ear. Veronica possibly isn't even coming; in addition to Catholic, she's likely a Buddhist—that's a religion where you practice not wanting anything by sitting cross-legged in the corner of your room for twenty minutes every day. Hector did it last year until his back gave out from the sitting, and on account he ended up dreaming and wanting more stuff than he ever knew was possible. Anyway, she's not going to want a fortune told by an amateur.

"In fact, Billy, we might forget about watching folks to get stuff to tell them at the carnival. At least for a while. We got to find out who is after you," I say, and I know I am serious about that.

We are walking to school, day two, with Georgie skipping along out front of us. He still hasn't figured out that school isn't fun and is looking forward to more of Miss Farisi and being an artist while being served up free crackers and milk. Rufus is ranging out beyond him scouting smells.

I notice Billy's face could be a field with dark clouds passing over it, and when he stops and looks at me there is some lightning crackling in his eyes too. I know why. It's 'cause his cheek is swollen up and yellow-blue and he doesn't want folks laughing at him. But I want to get him to tell me about his girl, if that's what she is, so I say, "That Chinese girl will still love you anyway, if she loved you in the first place." Little dust devils spin up in Billy's eyes, and he steps in front of me and hauls off and kicks me hard in the shin.

I sit down like dropped laundry and clutch my leg, gritting my teeth, the air hissing in and out of them. But Billy isn't through. He jumps on top of me and gets me in a neck lock and starts twisting until I fall onto my back, knocking my head on the sidewalk. Georgie is so little that he gets excited like an animal that doesn't know why it's fighting but will join in anyway and just jumps on me and starts punching me in the rib cage with his puny fists. Rufus piles on too, his big paws smashing my chest. It's Billy who has to pull them off.

I just lay flat on my back with my arms out to the sides and breathe hard. I don't want to beat up Billy unless I know why I am doing it, and I don't really want to beat him up, anyway. And right now Billy is so mad, I don't think I could manage it. But I make a note that in the future, Georgie will need some instruction on the matter of getting overexcited and punching persons, like myself, without invitation.

Billy holds Georgie by the neck like a mother cat will do one of its kittens until Georgie goes limp and he drops him. Rufus is stirred up and making slow circles around us. Billy starts signing at me so fast I almost can't keep up with him. *Stop telling me she is a* Chinese *girl. She is a girl. She is beautiful. Chinese has nothing to do with it, you idiot! That's like saying, Billy is that* deaf *kid, instead of just saying, That's that* kid, *Billy.*

I see what he means, and sudden, I feel low and mean and embarrassed as if I've had my jeans yanked down hard by some high school kid and my Fruit of the Looms are showing. And I don't know what to say. Which is awful. I know my face is looking sorrowful, but Billy thinks it's my Mrs. Ogilbee sorrowful and doesn't believe it and whips round and stomps off.

"Georgie," I say, "I think I messed up."

"That's okay, Paolo," he says. "You do it all the time."

"Georgie, when a person tells on themselves it ain't polite to agree with them in such an all-fired rush."

He takes a minute and thinks that over, then says slowly, "It isn't your fault you are ob nocth us."

"Obnoxious? Where the heck did you hear that?"

"Shawna told Margarita you are in seventh grade and can't help being it."

"Well, thank you for the information. And by the way, if Billy takes a mind to pounce on me, you stay out of it unless you're invited."

"Sure," he says. "Hey, are you going to walk me to school or should I walk myself, 'cause if I am going to walk myself, I'm going to run."

"Hold your horses, Georgie," I say, getting up, rubbing my shin. "You don't have to run."

"Then how am I going to get away from those guys coming for us from across the street?" He points, and I swing my head and see the Jensen clan coming our way.

The Jensen clan is two persons that are hill people from Porterville that came to live in Orange Grove about a year ago. They used to live in a cabin and smoke corncob pipes and hunt raccoons with their very own rifles. Even if you are four years old you get to have your own rifle if you are a Jensen. Hector told me raccoon is eatable. Ernie says it tastes like cat but wouldn't tell me how he knows about the taste of either.

The Jensens got reputations for being hotheads, and since they wear logging boots even to church no one wants to mess with them and get stomped mountain-style. Edgar is the oldest, ninth grade, and Jeffers is in fifth. They look exactly like each other except that Edgar is to the second power of Jeffers and has one eye that is cloudy and wanders to the left when he gets mad.

Right now that eye is locked hard left and the two of them are right there in my face. They don't touch me. They just look me over, Jeffers drooling some. I feel the joints in my knees getting watery and quivery. Georgie is standing behind me. Rufus is sitting on his haunches, tongue hanging, happy.

"Where's Billy?" Edgar says. He eyes Rufus, a bit cautious, the way everybody does. Rufus is big enough he could give pony rides for a nickel if he wasn't so lazy and liable to lie down and roll over and mash any little kid that was trying to ride him like he did Georgie when we tested.

"Billy, my cousin?"

"You know Billy who," Edgar says.

"You know Billy who," Jeffers says like a little echo. The both of them have overalls on and white T-shirts and are trying to grow blond mustaches that look like bleached-blond caterpillar legs sticking out above their lips.

"Billy, my cousin?" I repeat like I'm especially friendly and stupid, since I haven't figured out what to do next. They look at each other, as if they're looking into a mirror, scrunching their eyebrows down, decide I *am* stupid and switch attitudes.

"Yes, the Billy that lives with you," Edgar says, turning to me, and speaking slow and loud so I can understand him.

I smile and say, "Billy lives with my family."

They shake their heads at each other.

I smile, big.

"Well, you seen him this morning?" Edgar asks.

"Yes, he's at my house in the morning." I nod.

Edgar is having trouble talking to a stupid person without losing his temper. "Well, *where*, for example, is he right now this instant?"

"No . . . no, he's not here."

"He's at school," Georgie says.

Edgar and Jeffers take note of Georgie like he is pigeon poop just dropped out of the sky. Then they look at each other again, as is their way, and then they examine me again. Then all of a sudden Edgar jerks his jaw in the direction of Yosemite Elementary and John Muir Junior High, and they both turn on their three-inch Chippewa logging boot heels, the good kind 'cause hill people know boots, and they take off without saying one thing more to me or each other.

Georgie and I watch them go. Looking after them, I say, "Georgie, how come you told on Billy?"

"'Cause he is safe."

"How do you know that?"

"'Cause Billy is in his class with Mr. Bradshaw, which is too far down the hall from my class, room 407, so I don't have need of ever going over there and bothering him."

"How do you know Billy is already in there?"

"'Cause Billy is never late and is never going to be late on my account."

"What else did Billy tell you?" I say, looking over and down at him.

"Jensens don't like Billy hanging round Veronica."

My eyebrows shoot up at that.

"And Paolo."

"Yeah, Georgie?"

"I won't be able to walk to school with you if you make me late all the time."

9.

THAT'S RIGHT, BILLY SIGNS.

"How did you figure it out?" I say.

They follow her around.

"Hmm . . ."

Followed me walking her home once, I think. He blushes at that.

We are walking home slow, kicking mowed grass people have piled on the curb under their sycamores and maples that are planted all along the park strips. Georgie grabs handfuls and tosses them in the air, and we watch him as we go, sort of remembering, fond, of when we were young. All three of us cut just as lunch started so as not to have to bother with the Jensens until we have ourselves a plan to deal with them.

Billy looks downhearted, I believe, because his girl won't have him to take her home today. He got to see Veronica for a minute just as we were leaving campus. I'd gone over the fence to Yosemite Elementary to get him and Georgie right as the bell for lunch rang. She came out of her class with Billy. They didn't see me.

They came out slow, last ones out. "C'mon, you two, let's hustle," said Mr. Bradshaw, all smiles and genuine friendly, but also getting them out of his room so he could go eat. He locked the door and gave Veronica and Billy a thoughtful look, and then walked quickly down the hall. I decided to get a drink of water and had my lips pushed out trying to get a dribble from the water fountain just across from them. My eyeballs hurt from having them pegged hard-right to see those two while still getting some bubbles of rusty water.

Veronica was laughing at something Billy was trying to say with his hands. He put his notebook down on the ground and he wasn't using sign language, he was doing made-up stuff like in charades. His face was bright and warm-looking as a lightbulb and his eyes never left hers. Whatever it is was pleasing to her. She seemed a shy one, even her laughing seemed silent. Then he must have told her something more serious in that language they seem to have of their own, because she nodded her head in agreement and suddenly reached out and stopped his arms from moving, and then she brushed a bit of his hair away from his face. And they stayed stock-still like that, looking at each other until I started to look away, 'cause that little thing seemed very private.

But just then, a clump of girls, a half dozen or so, came around the corner laughing and talking, and they saw those two and they hushed up completely. But they stared at Veronica with poison-dart eyes while passing. And Veronica's face clouded up mad. Then I heard, "There you are!" A girl with straw blond hair was calling out from the end of the hall. She was smiling. *C'mon*, she waved. Veronica looked over at her and then back and nodded to Billy, a little smile slipping over her face, and he nodded, and she turned and trotted away toward her friend.

Now, walking with Georgie and Billy toward home, I'm still feeling a fool about seeing only that Veronica was Chinese and not seeing her the way Billy does, the way she is, a girl. What I'm keeping to myself and what's keeping me surprised over and over is that I see even if I thought she was a Commie, for sure, she'd still be a girl, and still Billy's girl at that.

For the first time, I think maybe I like this Commie stuff the way I like a scary movie. I only half believe it and only 'cause it gives me a thrill. Maybe I should really be scared about it. There's grown folks on the radio and such seem scared about it. I don't really know if I'm taking things too seriously or if I'm not taking them seriously enough. But looking at Billy now, I got to say, I know in my heart I am not scared of Veronica, and what you know in your heart has to count for something.

"You scared, Billy?"

No. Not really, he signs.

"We'll figure this out. We will." I don't know why but I don't say it must be the Jensens. I can tell he doesn't really care who broke his tooth on account he is so much thinking about her. I've already tried to get him to tell me exactly how they met, what it feels like to go goofy over a girl, what he thinks it costs to have a Chinese wedding. He's just ignored me.

We come to a halt in front of Mrs. Sweeney's house. "You know they owe you a tooth." I wonder to myself if "a tooth for a tooth" allows for us to get one from each of them. Maybe if we used algebra it would.

We've stopped because Georgie is stalking up to Mrs. Sweeney's picture window in broad daylight. Georgie hasn't figured out that Mrs. Sweeney is no longer a person of interest to us. She never threw no rock at Billy. And Mrs. Sweeney is right there on the front porch watching him, but Georgie doesn't see her. She's all perked-up and curious but quiet. He climbs right through her shrubbery and places his hands around his face, which he presses to her big front window. I figure I better come up with something so's my little brother doesn't get arrested for being a peeping Tom. "Georgie! We found her already! She's out on her front porch!"

Georgie's head goes up and he looks at me and then swings his head, slow, round where his eyes make a straight line to Mrs. Sweeney's eyes, which are looking down at him from up top her porch. He looks back at me like a trained dog and I feel proud of him. He doesn't budge nor say a thing and waits on me to make my move.

"Hi, Mrs. Sweeney!" I holler. "There you are. We were looking for you. We were wondering if you had a second or two?"

She doesn't say anything but just looks, not quite sure what's what.

Billy and I cross her lawn and I motion Georgie to come over too. He does.

"Mrs. Sweeney, we wanted to ask you about the French secret code from WWI. Mr. Sweeney gave it to us when we were kids, but we're not sure anymore if we have it right."

Now, mentioning Mr. Sweeney, who passed on a couple of years ago and is, in fact, the one who gave the code to Hector, is the very last thing she ever thought would come out of my mouth, and she doesn't know what to do or even say. She's a heavyset lady with a thousand wrinkles to her face, but still rosy and pink like the hairless baby moles I saw in one of her books once. Wrinkled but fresh. Her eyes are a blue that's all washed out, like old Levis, and she's just watching my mouth with them.

"Mr. Sweeney said he saw a French lance corporal use this code to run messages down the trenches once. The French . . . our allies," I add, since she still seems confused. Sometimes you have to go ahead and let people know what they are supposed to say next and now is one of those times. "We can show it to you, can't we? Right?" I go up her steps and my crew follows. Mrs. Sweeney is only about three inches taller than me once I'm up there with her. "I'll write it down and you can just check it. Okay?"

"Ah . . . all . . . right," she says softly. It sounds like a little girl is trapped somewhere down in her body and is doing the talking, whispering up through the pipe in her throat.

"Billy, paper."

Billy has his three-ring school binder, and he drops to one knee and tears off a sheet.

"Pencil."

He frowns up at me but opens his pencil pouch and hands one over. I lay things out on Mrs. Sweeney's big cement porch railing that's a foot wide and flat at the top and start sketching the code Billy and I have been using.

That little girl down in herself pipes up again. "You say that Arthur gave you a code from the war?"

"That's right, along with a trench coat and a leather holster with a flap he had in the garage." Hector told me that Mr. Sweeney had tired of him and Ernie going into that garage and going through his gear and finally just gave some of it to them. And once he'd got talking about the military, he'd given them the code. I guess being in the military isn't all it is cracked up to be. Pretty much it is saying, *"Yes, sir"* and sleeping in the mud and writing letters home saying, *Remember me?*

Mrs. Sweeney is watching over my shoulder, and Georgie is so close and watching with his mouth hanging open that he is drooling a bit on the corner of my paper. I sketch out the key to the code, including the letters:

ab	cd	ef
gh	ij	kl
mn	op	qr

st
uv wx
yz

Below that, I write my name in code and then write it out in alphabet letters underneath:

I step away and invite Mrs. Sweeney to take a closer look. "Well . . . well," is all she can say.

"See," I say. "If you want to spell 'Mrs.,' you draw the half box from the bottom left corner and leave out the two dots and that has to be the letter *M* and no other. To make the *R*, you draw the half box from the bottom right-hand corner and you include the two dots to show you mean *R*. Then, to show the *S*, you draw a big V shape and leave out the two dots. See?"

"Let me try that," she says, her hand out for the pencil.

I give it to her.

Carefully she scratches out the symbols. Then she writes the letters they represent underneath them, spelling out A-R-T-H-U-R. She stares at it for a good little while and then says, "That's . . . very clever, Paolo, but it looks . . . well . . . I don't . . . I don't think that would've fooled anyone in the military for long."

"Oh, sure it would."

I see Mrs. Sweeney's eyes are wet. "Paolo, that is something Arthur or one of his buddies made up themselves when they were bored. He was always doodling something."

I shake my head slowly and say, "I have it on the highest authority that this is a genuine French military code, Mrs. Sweeney." I am talking about myself and Hector.

"Well, that's sweet, Paolo. Arthur was an authority. In his way."

Billy motions to me.

I catch his meaning and ask, "Well, if this looks right to you, we'll get on home now."

"Well, it looks . . . right enough, I suppose." She seems a bit lonesome there on her porch in the middle of the day, thinking about Mr. Sweeney and the trenches and the French. Anyway, she's blinking back the sun or whatever it is that seems to be pecking at her eyes. "Has school let out already?" she asks, her whole self uncertain as she steps back and brushes her extra-black-hair-from-a-bottle back with one hand, and then dabs at her eyes with her palm, then crossing her arms like she's hugging herself.

"Oh, yeah, we had an assembly and they let us go early," I say.

Georgie's head is swinging back and forth watching and listening, but his hand goes up and slips the code off the cement and stuffs it in his pocket.

I get a hold of him lightly by his T-shirt and tug him after me down the steps. "Thanks awful much, Mrs. Sweeney," I say.

Billy nods polite-like.

We are heading down her walkway when she says, "Would you boys like to have any more of Mr. Sweeney's things?"

Georgie and I turn on our heels, sharp as sharp, like soldiers on parade, and Billy stumbles trying to catch up when he figures out we've made a U-turn and left him behind. In nothing flat we are in her garage, all of us nosed into an old trunk.

"I don't think that will ever fit you, Paolo." Mrs. Sweeney is handing me a green soldier shirt.

"Well, I won't need it until Halloween," I say.

"I seriously doubt you'll grow into it by then."

I shrug. I'm optimistic. Besides, I don't mind wearing things that are a little big for me. I do it all the time on account of having two older brothers. It is big, though; smells of dust and garage oil.

"Well, you won't want this," Mrs. Sweeney says, sighing and holding up a helmet that looks like a flat cooking pot, rusted so bad it has a jagged hole in it. By then we already know that Mrs. Sweeney has no idea what we'd want and what is a treasure and what isn't. I pull it, gentle but firm, from her hand, and she lets it loose 'cause she's got her eyes full of Georgie, who has the top half of his body into that trunk, as if he is going for a swim, arms paddling through all that gear, trying to get a good look at the stuff. He comes out with a thing that has a canister of some kind attached to a mask like a snout and big horse eyes made of yellow glass.

"Oh, gosh, how awful. That I am throwing out," she says.

Billy and I look at each other, trying to decide if we should argue or just fish it out of the trash later.

Georgie sees his chance and says, "I'll take it, Mrs. Sweeney."

"Oh, boys, really. Do you know what that is?"

We know it is the coolest piece of trash we've ever laid eyes on.

She shakes her head. "That is a gas mask. They used poison gas in that war. Just horrid, horrid, horrid."

Now we have got to have it. We let Georgie do the talking, since he can usually get whatever he wants from old folks 'cause he is little and cute to them.

"I'll take good care of it," he says.

She rears back her head as if he's said something nasty.

"I can bring it round for you to look at whenever you are missing it," he adds.

"Absolutely not," she says. "Just imagine what your mother would say."

"We won't show her," Georgie assures her.

"No." She snatches it from him and places it back in the trunk. "*That* will go in the trash. Oh, but here," she says. "Take this." She hands Georgie a leather belt that is brown with white spiderweb cracks. He forgets about the gas mask.

She ends up giving us about three-fourths of a uniform, a little trench shovel, and a scratchy blanket with moth holes in it that look the shape of the Big Dipper when you hold it up to the light.

"Well, that's about it," she says. "Maybe one of you can go as a soldier on Halloween."

"Mrs. Sweeney," I say, "Billy is thinking of going as a Chinaman. You wouldn't happen to have anything along those lines?"

She looks at me like I'm the wonder I am but says, "I think it is time you all went along home now."

Which is true, since Billy has grabbed a bit of the flesh on my back with his fingers and is twisting it hard and also since we have to get home before Rufus takes off for school looking for us *and* so we can come back and get that gas mask.

10.

"I'M TELLING YOU," I SAY TO GEORGIE AND Billy, "since we left school early, I don't think it would be good to have Mom know that and get more stress than she needs."

Right, okay, right, Billy signs.

"Mom's not home," Georgie says.

"Says who?"

"I says," Georgie says.

"Georgie, you know as much about where Mom is as Rufus knows about church."

"She's *at* church."

I stop, hold up my arm like a cavalry scout. I realize he's right. Mom is over at the church 'cause it's Tuesday. Her Ladies Altar Society does their bit on Wednesday nights, but when they have extra problems they go in Tuesdays. Today they are putting new candles in for folks to light and wish on and pray. I heard her say so myself a couple days back.

"Well, that means we can go see Uncle Charlie about how to train Rufus."

Billy scrunches his eyebrows like worms arching their backs.

"Train him to do what?" Georgie asks.

"To be an attack dog and keep those Jensens off us."

Both Billy and Georgie's mouths drop open and their eyes spark like little thistles of fire and they smile. They are again impressed, as they should be, at my smarts and my cunning. I believe I'd make an excellent Red Chinese, if I cared to.

I let Billy and Georgie be respectfully impressed by me for a bit, which I can tell they are by the fact they leave their mouths hanging open. Either that, or they are waiting for me to say something interesting before we scoot home and find Uncle Charlie as expected out on our front porch. He hears me out polite enough but says right off, though slowly, "Not a good idea." Uncle Charlie uses words like they arc quarters and he doesn't have need of giving them away, and if he does have to give them, he has all day to do it, which he has since he doesn't work. He lives with us on account he got his lungs ruined mining coal in West Virginia and also from drinking a case of Hamm's beer every twenty-four hours.

My dad lets him live in a room in the attic, and if he isn't up in it, he's on the front porch in a big easy chair he had us drag out there for him. He likes watching traffic and studying on clouds and telephone wires and such. My dad says we are not to grow up and take after him. Says it's okay for Uncle Charlie to go on with his black-sheeping on account of all he's seen in his life during the war way down the bottom of the world in the South Pacific, but we are supposed to be good sheep, bright as bleached laundry.

"Why isn't it such a good idea?" I ask. I know I have to ask, since he won't tell and spend one word more than he has to.

Uncle Charlie sucks his lips in the way persons do who have store-bought teeth they've forgot to put in. Uncle Charlie has the most beautiful teeth in Orange Grove City. He's got large ears that cock out from the sides of his head, which is long and skinny, so his teeth, which are big as a mule's, set things off especially nice. He leaves them out most of the time, since they are so large they hurt him. Right now he slips them out of his shirt pocket, pops them in, and smiles.

We all smile back 'cause we always enjoy watching that, and Uncle Charlie will usually do it for us as many times as we like if he doesn't have too much of a hangover. This morning he looks a little wobbly. He's mule-starved skinny and has bones so thin I imagine them brittle as dead sticks of bamboo.

"Well, Paolo," he says. "Suppose we train Rufus like you want him, he gets overexcited, you forget how to handle him—dog could end up biting one of your friends."

"We don't have friends," Georgie says.

"That's right," I say.

Billy nods his head too.

"On account we have enough persons in our family for company," Georgie says.

We all shake our heads in agreement, assuring Uncle Charlie we have no worries in the friends department.

He smirks and snorts once and it starts him coughing, his chest rattling like a leather bag full of marbles. But he keeps eyeing us, adding and subtracting something in his head. He wouldn't waste words talking it out. It's time for us to practice virtue. This time, Patience—which is just a name for being stuck and having no choice about it and so call it patience and call attention to it if you get a chance so as to be admired. Also it makes you feel less a fool to think you are in control of something, even if that something is only your thoughts, so

I recommend that virtue. By the way, what I'm saying to you now is Generosity.

Even though he's said what he's said, we are still hopeful on account we know Uncle Charlie could train a dog better than anyone, 'cause when he was in the Philippines he had a Doberman pinscher of the rank of a corporal in the Marines that he used to sniff out enemies that liked to hide in these badger holes they'd dug all over the jungle.

He looks at us with his watery gray eyes and reaches down to the side of his chair and comes up with a can of Hamm's he slurps on while keeping his eyes on us, still deciding what he's going to do.

"Rufus wouldn't bite anyone we didn't tell him to," Georgie says.

Uncle Charlie puts his beer down and takes out a pack of Camels nonfilters, shakes one loose into his hand. He's got hands soft as oil. Hamm's beer will make your hands like that and your skin so thin you can see little threads of blood veins all over your face. Make it look like the cracks in those old paintings of folks I saw at a museum once.

Uncle Charlie lights up with a chromium Ronson cigarette lighter he snaps open and shut with a snap of his wrist, sucks the poison in, and blows it out slow with some kind of relief and deep pleasure, picks a bit of tobacco off his lip with his thumb and forefinger and flicks it away. "Okay," is all he says.

"All right!" I shout, throwing my hands up. Then I get control of myself, since if you act too excited it worries grown-ups unnecessarily.

Georgie scoots off the porch and comes back, lickety-split, with Rufus, who immediately collapses as if he was one of those hundred-pound sacks of pinto beans my mom buys once every year. Rufus never misses a chance to rest.

Uncle Charlie looks down at him, says, "This ought to be interesting." That surprises me, since that is a dollar-and-a-quarter sentence, and he could have said the same thing for free by just grunting. He must want the job and our company, and I'd give him a hug right now, except I'm afraid I'd snap bones doing it.

11.

M<small>OM</small> <small>CAME HOME, MADE OURS AND EVERY-</small>
body's dinner, left us to eat it, went upstairs to do ironing. She
didn't bother us, said she was overtired, said just, "Eat. Eat."

It's seven o'clock and dark by the time we get to Mrs.
Sweeney's garage. We have to give up good time we could be
using to find out if it was the Jensens who busted Billy's tooth,
but we know we got to get the rest of that army gear tonight or
else it might go out in the garbage and we'll miss our chance.

We spent the afternoon with Uncle Charlie training Rufus.

He decided we could only have an alarm dog and not an attack one. Said it was safer all around and that Rufus was so big that that should be all we need. An alarm dog is one that will start up barking and growling and curling its lips back when you clear your throat and leave off doing it when you say, "Tsk." Do "Tsk" sharp, with your tongue against your teeth.

Here's what you do to get an alarm dog. You get Rufus on a leash, the kind that is chain and will snap up with a harsh noise. It's the noise that gets the dog's attention, not the strangling like most people think. You only got to strangle once and it's not even a real strangle and a dog with normal smarts will know ever after that the sound of the chain being snapped almost-tight means, *Stop doing whatever you are doing.*

Some people are so ignorant they think it is cruel to do that, when actually a dog likes knowing you are in charge. That way they can relax and let you run things and not have to bother about it themselves. Same is true of kids, now I think of it. I know that a kid will make a stink sometimes when his folks won't let him do something he wants, but I know also that a kid who has folks that won't go to the trouble of making him do as they say can start to hate on them.

I've seen that happen. And I believe it. I believe those kids hate them 'cause down deep they feel afraid knowing they have to be in charge of themselves. And 'cause they get to suspecting their folks don't care enough to go to the bother of seeing their own kid obey them. Anyway, that's just what I think and it might or might not be true, and you are free to decide for yourself. There's no reason you can't think for yourself, even if you have somebody smarter than most to do your thinking, as I've done. But what can't be doubted is that Rufus enjoyed his alarming and took to it right off.

First, Uncle Charlie sliced up a hot dog into twenty pieces. Then he had Rufus sit in front of him. Rufus wanted those pieces quivery bad, and when he realized Uncle Charlie wasn't going to give them, he got frustrated. Started to whine and then, finally, he barked. Now the second he barked, Uncle Charlie cleared his throat with a little growl and slipped Rufus a bit of wiener.

Then they'd start all over. Rufus would get mad 'cause Uncle Charlie wouldn't just hand over the treats, and again, finally, he'd bark, and Uncle Charlie would growl quick and give the meat. It took forever for Rufus to connect the little growling in the back of Uncle Charlie's throat to the barking and the treat. But the second he got it, he was wild with that knowledge. He'd wait on Uncle Charlie, his eyes keen as a wolf's, his neck stretched forward, drool forming up and dangling down from the side of his lip like a rosary made out of clear glass.

The very second Uncle Charlie did his throat growling,

Rufus would bark and get his little wafer of hot dog and go right back to watching and waiting and eyeing Uncle Charlie like a pointer dog that'll stiffen when it smells a bird in the brush.

Well, next you put Rufus on his leash and you walk him up and down the block, and when you pass by your house, Uncle Charlie comes out with a broom he shakes while he's shouting and playing like he's mad. When he comes close, I do the throat growl and Rufus starts barking, and right that second, Uncle Charlie acts afraid and backs up quick as he can, which isn't that quick actually, though it'll do and it did.

I give Rufus his treat and start barking and growling too, so as to encourage Rufus to get worked up. Uncle Charlie goes back and forth at us with the broom until Rufus is barking and straining at his leash and playing he is going to have Uncle Charlie for lunch. Then when you want Rufus to knock it off, all you have to do is snap the chain and say, "Tsk." You let yourself go kind of limp and say cooing things to Rufus and give him another treat, and while Uncle Charlie backs away, Rufus settles down, satisfied with his new power.

I couldn't have trained Rufus to do it even if I knew how, but Uncle Charlie has a knack for understanding dog thinking, and we got the whole thing done in two hours. Billy and Georgie learned it too. Billy was pleased since all he had to do was growl and *tsk* and not talk words.

So we have Rufus with us and the moon riding our shoulders like a pal and are all of us working our fingers into the sliding wood door of Mrs. Sweeney's garage so we can get it open and ourselves in.

We put ourselves to the job and the door begins a slow slide to the right, rusted and complaining with a dull squeak all along the track it is set on with little wheels like they have on skates. I'm afraid that noise will fetch Mrs. Sweeney or even Mr. Koski, if he's come calling again. I'm pretty sure now Mrs. Sweeney never called the FBI on Mr. Koski or anybody else. She's too nice, and she's lonesome, has need of Mr. Koski's company. What Hector said about Ernie pulling my leg on that one seems the truth. But she'd call the cops if she thought burglars were in her garage. We get the door open quiet as possible, enough for us to squeeze in, popping sweat even though the night air has started to get some cool to it. I turn on my flashlight and flick it round the room like a fly fisherman's rod until it drops on the old chest.

We waste no time getting the gas mask and one more soldier's shirt, and at the bottom of the trunk, we find a thick wool jacket that snaps at the neck with a stand-up collar. It's got old brass buttons and is supposed to go down about a half foot below your waist and be belted there. On me it goes to my knees, but it looks way more cool than any coat I've ever known and I take it.

We have everything loaded in pillowcases we brought for that purpose and are getting ready to leave when we hear Rufus whining. I shine the light in the direction of his whimpers, and there he is nosing at what looks like a closet door in the corner of the garage.

We tiptoe over. Georgie clamps on Rufus's mouth to hush him. I point the flashlight at Billy's face and he nods what I know means, *Yes, let's look.*

I unwind Rufus's leash from where I have it lashed round my waist and hook him up. I make Georgie go over to the door in case we have to make a run for it, though I can't think of what is on the other side of the door except maybe a couple of rats having a party. I switch off my flash and turn the knob, careful, quiet as I can.

I push the door open a crack and a thin sheet of light slips out through the opening. I have one eye peeking, but there are two eyes looking dead-certain back. Those eyes are Mr. Koski's. He's sitting at a little table in a room there just then lighting his pipe with a wooden match, sitting there with a ham radio set that is crackling alive like a brain with who-knows-how-much knowledge. Mr. Koski's eyes are flung wide like window shades that've snapped up, sudden-sharp.

Who the heck would've thought I'd have use of an alarm dog the very same day I got one, that I didn't even have to set him growling and spitting like he was wolf-wild mad, that Mr. Koski would be so startled he'd fall back over the little metal stool he was sitting on, sparks from his pipe knocked loose like little comets, that I'd catch a Commie, totally red-handed like that.

12.

WE DON'T RUN HOME. We run to San Joaquin Cathedral, where Billy and I are altar boys and where they are open Tuesday and Saturday nights for confessions. At our church you have to say your sorrys to a priest and then he'll square things for you. You can't just say sorry to God, direct. It would be disrespecting of the priest profession and not do at all. Though if you are a pagan you can go on and talk to God or whomever you please and you can still get in heaven on account of Mercy.

It's not so much we are in need of confession, but we are too spooked to go home without somebody noticing our nerves, and we need somewhere safe in case Mr. Koski is following us, which he may very well be doing. He drives round in a red Dodge panel truck that looks likes an ambulance with no windows. Uses it to do all his biology collecting and camping and, I guess, his spying.

Since he fell over himself and his stool, and we lit out of there so fast, we don't know if he saw us well enough to know exactly who we are. Rufus was barking and snarling, mostly out of surprise, not anger, which is not his way at all, but only his head was poked through that door, and how would Mr. Koski recognize a dog just by seeing its tongue and its teeth?

Then again, on account he is a biologist, he might be able to do just that. Biologists make a business out of looking at a bird or a leaf or the bark of a tree and then looking up in a book to see if it actually is a bird or a leaf or bark. It is more fun than it sounds, 'cause they go camping all the time and have a ready-made reason to get out of the house whenever they want without their wives getting after them, though Mr. Koski himself isn't married. If I wasn't already set on being a newspaperman—which is a job like no other on account you can drive round talking to folks, snapping pictures all day, and even get to close up Murphey's Place every night with your buddies—I might go in for biology-style camping myself.

We go right up the long steps they have and into one of the eight doors out front of the cathedral, let Rufus loose to ramble, which means he falls asleep on those steps and waits on us. Just before we go in, I say to Billy, "So you still think I'm acting a fool?"

And even us catching a Communist like we did and all of us running all the way here, Billy still gives me a questioning look, lips puckered up, and shrugs his shoulders.

"We'll see," is what I say, shaking my head.

"Paolo, I want to light a candle," Georgie says as we are walking down the main aisle, enjoying the warmth and the soft buttermilk light and the pictures on the ceiling and all round. Billy and I know the pictures by heart: John the Baptist, skinny from eating grasshoppers and honey, pouring a little clamshell full of water on Jesus; Michael the Archangel, stepping on Lucifer's head and driving a spear through his big black bat wings and his spine; a hundred little fat-bottomed baby angels holding up a cloud that has Jesus going up like he's riding an elevator to heaven; and our favorite, which is St. Patrick pointing his finger like Uncle-Sam-I-Want-You at a thousand snakes that are all wriggling and leaping and slithering to get off this rock that is supposed to be Ireland.

Gives us the shudders just to look. Church is way better than any scary movie.

Georgie is over where the candles are all racked and glowing like glass tubes of an old radio. Billy and I slide up next to him. "Who you lighting candles for, Georgie?"

He looks at me, his lips like a coin purse snapped tight. He knows lighting candles is like a birthday wish and you don't have to tell. He takes one of his quarters and slips it into the little money box they got there for paying, gets the little sticks for lighting and touches five of the nickel candles awake, each with its own little hope.

"I should think a couple of those are for me and Billy," I say.

Georgie looks at me. He's not saying, but he suddenly looks a little worried. He drops his other quarter into the box and lights five more.

Billy opens his eyes wide in admiration.

"Maybe Georgie is going to be the one who grows up to be a priest," I mouth whisper-like at Billy.

He nods with satisfaction.

If you have a big Catholic family, one of your sons is supposed to grow up to be a priest, and everybody is always pestering you about it and wondering which one will give up on women and living in a regular house with evenings and weekends off.

Just then I hear a rustling coming up on us and then hear

Monsignor's voice. "You better come on, now. I was about to lock up. But I've got time for two more confessions," he says, nodding at me and Billy.

We have no other excuse for being there, so we follow him slow but going like prisoners heading off to be shot. He's already to the confessional. That's a man-sized closet where the priest sits in a big chair with the door closed. Those that are in need of confessing go into a small closet next to his. The priest has a little window made out of wood with a hundred holes the size of nails drilled into it so you can talk to him without him seeing just exactly who you are. Just 'cause you have to tell on yourself, it's not to shame you.

Billy's deaf, so as usual, Monsignor leaves the door to his closet open, hands Billy a little white notepad, where Billy stands and writes down his stuff. It never takes them long. Monsignor just reads what he's written, nods, and blesses him. Billy always comes away from there pretty chipper. I think he likes the attention, and the truth is Monsignor is an Irishman priest with cheeks the color of persimmons and a bald head who is all the time good to us, and we are genuine fond of him.

Georgie doesn't have to go to confession, 'cause he's not seven yet and so can't understand when he is doing bad or not, which isn't the whole truth if you ask me. Georgie pretty much knows right from wrong; it's just that he does mostly right, since it is his nature. I'm not sure about my nature. It has some right and wrong in it but in between a hundred other things I have no names for. They do remind me of St. Patrick's snakes, though.

When Billy is done, I go in. I don't think this is exactly fair on account no one is supposed to know who is the one confessing, yet Monsignor giving us our own special invite has made my person known. But I can't see any way out of it and go on and do the best I can.

"Bless me, Father," I start, and then a bunch of other stuff you say before you get to the main event, which is ratting on yourself. My problem, right now, is I have nothing to tell. I have been good as far as I know. But Monsignor will never buy that and will just make me stay there till I come up with something.

"I . . . had hateful thoughts . . . about my sisters and . . . about Corky Diller," I manage.

"Umm."

"I . . . twisted Georgie's ears without his permission."

"Uh-huh."

"I shot our neighbor's windows out with my BB gun, and . . . and . . . I buried my sister's wig, took a case of Uncle Charlie's Hamm's beer to school, and have plans to drown Alfred, our cat." Once I start, I find I like confessing.

"Paolo, lad," Monsignor says, all Irish weariness there in his voice.

"Yes, Father."

"You have an affliction."

"I do?"

"You're too fond of the sound of your own voice." And then, like a judge when he knocks his little hammer down and gives out your sentence, he says, "Seventeen Our Fathers."

Then I see his shadow leave his closet, and I am there alone to say the prayers I've been told to say. I think that since I am going to be a newspaperman, there is no sin in practicing my stories, but if I were to think of the church like the Mafia, then Monsignor is a kind of godfather and if not that, he is, at the least, juiced-in way more than me, so I just can't risk going against him. I do the seventeen right there on the spot.

When Billy was done I noticed he had no penance, no prayers he had to say. I think a guy ought to be able to come out of the church closet without having to do his penance in front of the whole wide world. I do them right inside there and I get them all done in four minutes flat, which is about fourteen seconds each, if my math is right. That's virtue—in this case, a willingness to work hard, which is called Industry. And the Lord knows I have it.

*　　　*　　　*

"Paolo," Georgie says, "are we going to tell the FBI on Mr. Koski?"

We are walking the twelve blocks home, just rambling and taking our time and enjoying the silky blue sky and the cooling night breeze that comes in through the mountain passes in California this time of year. "Well . . . sure, but not right off," I say.

"How come?"

"We need more evidence, and we need to know who else in Orange Grove is part of his bunch." I don't say also that Mr. Koski is an usher at San Joaquin Cathedral and knows everybody in town, and how could he be like everyone in town and be in need of reporting to the FBI? You can't go reporting *everybody*—unless it's necessary, I guess. I don't really know. I do know it would spoil all our fun for this year if we were to let the FBI do what we can do ourselves.

"Do you think we'll get our pictures in the paper?" Georgie asks.

"Might."

"Rufus, too?"

"Probably not."

"How come not?"

"'Cause he is too big and would take up the whole picture and on account he is not an official police dog."

"He's not?"

"No, he is not."

"Why not?"

"You have to be trained by the police and not by your uncle who lives in the attic, and you have to be German." That takes care of Georgie for a while 'cause it is more information than he can handle, and he is walking all around those words trying to make them hook up like little railroad cars in a sentence in his head that could huff up to his brain, like I-think-I-can-I-think-I-can, loaded heavy with what I said.

I am not interested in having my picture in the paper, since Ernie has always told us that our goal is to stay out of trouble and *not* end up on the front page of the paper, which he thinks we won't be able to help doing one of these days, so when it happens we have instructions to give a name other than O'Neil.

All of a sudden Rufus starts up his alarm-dog barking. I look over at Billy. He's tugging on Rufus's chain, so I say, "Tsk." That should hush him limp, but it doesn't. He's straining and barking and looking off into the dark. We look then too. Look and see it ain't dark at all. See the sky way over and gone behind our house is glowing like a huge dome. Watch the world and the clouds and the bits of leaves riding the wind rushing past us, 'cause by then we're running, full-out, toward home.

13.

THOSE FLAMES ARE SLIPPING UP THE TRUNK of our oak like thousands of tiny goldfish wriggling hard toward heaven. When they reach the undersides of the floorboards of our tree house, they turn into orange-blue and black snakes slipping and winding up it, lurching over the short walls and into it, their little tongues flickering, and then—big barrels of smoke roll off the top of that oak, showing black as oil against the sky that is moon-soaked and bright.

"Get back, Georgie!" I shout. Little explosions are going off up there high, showering down, like someone is seeding the dark, scattering it, and the air hissing too.

Billy goes, slow, to his knees in the soft orchard dirt, head back and rocking, which I've never seen and so know he is heart-shook, serious and for real. Georgie is jaw-dropped and I think almost enjoying the sight of it, not old enough to be scared of the power there is in this world, the power we can see now was always there but not showing. But once you see it, you know ever after it's there and could unloose itself when it wills, like it is doing now in big flashing sheets of fire.

And suddenly, there is Hector and my grandpa Leonardo and all my sisters and then Ernie hollering us all back, and us reminding me of some kind of dark tribe standing in a harbor somewhere in the South Seas, like I think I read in Hector's Robert Louis Stevenson book, watching the masts of a ship burn and collapse. Clumps of leaves and mistletoe are burning and tearing away like small sails, the sky snapping with large and small flags of flame.

Pretty soon both Orange Grove City fire trucks come bumping up the little ranch road that is a border to that orchard of almonds. They even leapfrog out through four rows of the little trees till the dirt is too soft and the trucks slump down like old dinosaurs in movies, making those same herky-jerky motions and growling, all fury and frustration.

But they are close enough they can get water they suck into hoses from a small ditch out there and shower it up over our tree house until the fire finally sizzles out. Mostly it has burned itself out anyway, and the watering just keeps the sparks from spreading to the almonds.

Not long and there is just a big, quiet stump stabbing up—a giant black crayon stuck in the ground—and the ground around it just pebbles of bark all charred and traced in red and that red taking the firemen the longest time to erase with their hoses shooting water.

Fire chief Captain Jack Branigan shows my grandpa a box of kitchen matches his men have found, and he is pointing out where it is they picked it up and then he is pointing *at me.*

"No, sir," I say when they ask. "Never was a time *ever* we played with matches." I think I sound false, and I see my grandpa looking at me like he's about to cry, though he'd not do that in front of men. Grandpa thinks of himself as American, 100 percent, and why not? He is 100 percent, but he thinks there are some that wouldn't agree and would see him as I-talian and nothing more, and he doesn't want anyone thinking he or any of his would do a thing to hurt the U. S. of A.

Ernie and Hector are talking low to themselves and eyeing me and Billy, evil. Georgie goes over to Captain Jack and pulls on his big yellow sleeve and says, "Paolo didn't do it."

The captain looks down at Georgie and says, "That so?"

"Yep," Georgie says with a nod of his head, sincere like he always is.

"Well, who did?"

He motions the captain to come close and when he goes down on one knee and cocks his head so as to listen, Georgie covers his mouth with his little chubby hands, but I hear him anyway when he whispers, "Communists."

14.

NEXT DAY MY DAD COMES HOME AND WE
have the longest session of our lives. If my head was a house
then it is two stories, and he takes it apart one board at a time,
every one of those nails yelping when he pries it loose, them
coming out reluctant and bent. After inspecting it all, he stacks
each bit in its own spot.

He never throws any of the lumber down nor stomps on
any. Instead he goes slow and so careful it makes me feel guilty
for all the trouble he's going to. I'm glad my dad knows that

sessions go with the job of dad—he's never held them against me. But it is the first time I feel unsure about the advantages of being a newspaperman and known for being partial to sentences of my own design, the kind that are inspired by the truth rather than tied to it.

My dad is chock-full of virtue. He's especially Determined; though sometimes I think Determined is a first cousin to Stubborn. But he puts me back together and there are no pieces left over like there was once when we assembled a model airplane that came in a box. Kind of makes you nervous when you build something and it looks fine but there are pieces, extra, that should've gone somewhere. Anyway, all my self is in place, though I admit I feel a little loose and shaky, and know I'll have to do some tightening of things on my own.

Georgie saved me. He got a session just before mine that lasted only five minutes and that I overheard 'cause I had my ear glued to the keyhole. Even though Dad quizzed me good, I know after his talking to Georgie he didn't really want the whole story. Leastways, that is my guess. "Georgie," my dad says, "did you boys set that tree on fire?" My dad can beat around a bush longer than the average dad if he cares to, but he does not care to today.

"Nope," Georgie says. I hear him yawning. He's sleepy, since he's been up most of the night like the rest of us.

"Think carefully, son. Did you or Paolo or your cousin Billy light any matches—maybe by accident? I know you boys loved that tree house and wouldn't burn it on purpose."

"Nope." I can imagine Georgie shaking his head like he does when he knows what the question you are asking him means and he knows, right off, the answer.

"Did you see anyone other than Billy or Paolo or you light matches?" The firemen and everyone made a big deal out of those kitchen matches, and it's been all over town—who would do it, use matches like that on purpose to start fires?

"No, sir," Georgie says. "You could cut a switch and beat me if you want," he adds, kind of hopeful. My grandma Leonardo is always threatening us she will do that, though no one in my family has ever laid a hand on us, much less a switch. I suppose Georgie wouldn't think it would be fun if they had.

My dad doesn't say anything to that.

And then Georgie tells him the whole truth of things just like he had to tell Captain Jack. "Mr. Koski and the Communists lit that tree on fire."

"Hmm . . . yes. That's what I heard." A little doubt or annoyance crawling into my dad's voice. "Who exactly told you that, Georgie?"

"No one had to tell me."

"Why is that?"

"There are Communists all over Orange Grove. Ask Paolo. Him and me and Billy are helping the FBI catch them."

"You know that's plain nonsense, don't you? There is such a thing as Communism, but you're not going to find it in the cupboards."

Georgie doesn't say anything, so I imagine he's thinking first chance he gets, he's going down to the kitchen and check there.

"I guess I am going to have to limit the time you boys spend listening to the radio."

"We saw the radio, we didn't listen to it," Georgie says.

"*Saw* the radio. What? Son. Well . . . *who* do you listen to?"

"Hector. And Ernie."

My dad blows out a big spurt of relief. "Well, now, see, that ought to tell you right there what you're hearing just may be coming from . . . three degrees left of Pluto," Dad says, his voice all dryness.

There is a little pause, and I give what he said some thought and think that I am going to have to put more consideration on it later.

Then there's doubt or annoyance in his voice at Georgie not understanding, when my dad sighs and says, "Anything else you want to tell me?"

"Billy has a Chinaman girlfriend."

"A what?"

"A Chinaman—"

"Okay, stop." He waits a half minute and says, "You mean a girl he is fond of is Chinese."

"That's what I said," Georgie explains.

"Hmm . . . ," my dad says, to himself.

Georgie asks, "It's okay we work with the FBI?"

My dad answers right back, quick. "Well, could be Mr. Hoover will be grateful, but don't get your heart set on it." He says it serious, maybe him not wanting to shame Georgie for thinking him to be certifiably out of his mind. Either that or under the age of reason, like Monsignor thinks: too ignorant to know what he's doing yet.

And that's the thing about the bald truth, and why I've never been especially fond of it—no one's interested.

15.

It's good to live in a town like Orange Grove. Everybody knows everyone or is related to them 'cause of someone's sister marrying somebody's cousin. That's supposed to make for idiot kids with fish fingers or monkey tails and the like, but in my case it means that Captain Jack knows my dad by some distant blood relation—so Captain Jack believed him and us and let the whole tree house fire drop. They called it accidental arson. If it was on-purpose arson it would get you ten years in juvenile hall, where you'd have to eat white bread and butter sandwiches and get tears tattooed on your cheek and walk with an ankle-chain shuffle the rest of your life.

It was the Jensens, Billy signs to me. He's been signing that for more than two weeks now. We're walking home from school and he's just signed it again. *Or whoever threw that rock. It's somebody who doesn't want me to see Veronica.*

I tell him, "I still say it could have been Mr. Koski on account he uses kitchen matches for his pipe and was the one who was the most recent mad at us."

Billy shakes his head. *We don't even know if Mr. Koski saw us either of those times,* he spells, fingers moving like a trumpet player with no horn. I think Billy has been depressed the last two weeks. Dad said we had to stick close to home for two weeks or so, just for good measure, even though the fire wasn't our fault. All we've been doing is going to school and doing altar boys at church every other Sunday. Things are so bad we've even been doing our homework.

"Billy, Veronica talks to you at school. And I know since Georgie tells me he sees that you two go off by yourself on a bench at lunch, so you got no reason to be blue." What I want is for him to tell me why exactly he is so blue. He still has his Veronica, and we realized the Jensens can't get to him at school 'cause of Coach Morton walking around both our schoolyards and keeping kids from fighting.

Coach Morton was a boxer once. Has the nose of a thumb to prove it. Still shrugs his shoulders like he's loosening up for a right or left cross every time he speaks. He calls the boys ladies and thinks he is especially clever for it, though he's said it one hundred thousand times and no one has ever laughed or is even insulted by it anymore.

I've had good teachers, but in some cases, maybe being a teacher is just living in your own world and talking to yourself and getting paid for doing it. Ernie says that is the way it is for everyone, really. That the world is mostly in your head—the trick is to consider yourself the star of your movie and to write your own reviews. Just take care that some persons agree with you. Or at least try to be pleasant enough so folks will be pleasant back, not talk too much during your movie.

He said to be careful, though, about teachers and parents always telling you that you can grow up to be anything or anyone you want to be. Says up at Stockton State Mental Hospital they have two Napoleons, a Paul Revere, and a lady that is more alley cat than not. He said in his opinion the way I'm going he thinks I might turn out to be an actor. Or a sheep. Said in the basement of the college up at Stanford they actually have a little boy in a big pickle jar that is half boy, half sheep. I know it is true, but it's spooky—sometimes I'd prefer Ernie not take as much care as he does about my education.

"When can we do the FBI'ing again, Paolo?" Georgie says. He has Rufus on his chain, Rufus looking out for us, walking us home every day 'cause the Jensens are scared of him. Georgie is looking at Rufus's head, which is near level to his own. Those two love each other as much as two persons can. He looks Rufus right in the eye and Rufus looks back, even though dogs are said to never look you in the eye. I'm glad Georgie has a friend, and I'm glad he's asked what he has. It's what I've been mad to do myself for exactly the last sixteen days but not been able to get Billy interested in.

"Billy," I say, "Mr. Koski lit that fire as sure as we are walking here, right now. If we were to catch him with some proof of his spying we could have something to remember the rest of our lives."

Billy watches my lips, but his eyes don't spark.

"The worst that could happen is he could box us up some night and ship us to Russia or shoot us with a poison dart and bury us in his basement, and . . . that just won't happen. Well . . . probably it won't."

Billy lets out a smirk of a smile, which makes me brighten a bit.

Georgie butts in. "Paolo, if you are going as a soldier on Halloween, I was thinking I would go as a papier-mâché tank."

"No kidding," I say. "What gave you that idea?"

"Miss Farisi is fond of papier-mâché, and it would take her all day to do me up over her house."

"Oh . . ." Georgie is not stupid, but he is too little to be embarrassed that by now everybody in town knows he's planning on marrying Miss Farisi the very second he's grown enough he can fit a man-sized tux.

We are just now coming up on our house and we round the corner and walk into our yard. We stop 'cause shouting at us in big red letters, spray-painted on the wood siding of our garage is, STAY AWAY FROM THAT LITTLE CHINA DOLL! Right in the flowerbed beneath that somebody who is trying hard to be a genuine devil has left a box of kitchen matches. One match is out of the box and pushed in, careful, so that it is standing up in the soil.

16.

YES, BILLY SIGNS. *Yes, every other day or so. People you wouldn't imagine. Not many, but enough. Yes, talking trash. Saying I should stick to my own kind. Yes, that is exactly why I've been downhearted.*

We've run out by our burnt tree to talk. I guess, technically, we are runned-away again, part-time. I check my watch. It's only four thirty. We got plenty of time to get home for our Friday-night dinner. We eat burgers made from some kind of fish mash from cans on Fridays, and with plenty of ketchup, it's not bad. "Well . . . kitchen matches or not, Mr. Koski doesn't care who your girlfriend is or isn't. He wouldn't write that." I feel my head is a basketball and the air has just been let out of it. I mumble to myself, "Could mean, then, he didn't do arson, either. Heck, I don't know."

Billy reads my lips and nods in agreement.

"You know that kids talking trash at school are just being ignorant, Billy," I say. "Ain't any different from the way I talked before you explained things to me."

I can't go around punching them. Billy gives emphasis to a word by pushing his eyes out, bug-eyed, when he's signing it.

"No one is saying you should. I'm only saying don't take it to heart." Billy is no sissy, and yet this thing has got him red-eyed, shoulder-slumped, and breathing all jerky like a windup toy that's on its last couple of clicks.

"Billy," Georgie says, touching him on the elbow, "Miss Farisi says we are all the same color."

"Yeah, what's that?" I ask.

"The color *human*."

Billy squints hard at Georgie, maybe trying not to cry, maybe not.

Georgie nods his head and pats Billy's elbow. Rufus slides up and gives the side of Billy's head a huge lick that leaves his hair standing up on one side. Billy looks impressed by what we're saying. He lets out a big sigh.

He and I glance at each other and I know it is going to be all right. We've always been able to figure our way out of things as good as we can figure ourselves into them. Why not this time?

17.

"THIS-A IS-A NO GOOD," GRANDPA LEONARDO
is saying. It's Saturday morning and everyone but my dad, who
is gone on his train, has seen the sign, shook their heads, and
wandered off, leaving us to take care of our own business the
way we do in our family. When you got more than a dozen
people living in your house, it's too hard to keep up on everyone's affairs. It's kind of like living in an apartment building, I
think. And they know Grandpa is riled about it. It's not the
kind of thing he walks away from. "This-a is-a America," he

says, his jaw pushed out and his lower lip sticking out, fat. I end up telling him about Veronica and Billy, and that makes his eyes burn mad.

"Billy can-a talk-a to whose-a ever he want. This-a is-a America." He's slashing the air like Zorro or your average Italian grandpa.

He keeps saying that, shaking his head, sounding like he is determined for America to be the way it's supposed to be—free and fair for everybody. Hector told me once that America was only as good as the folks in it and that those folks had to make themselves right all over again every generation. A generation is like your grandparents; they are one generation, then your folks, and that's another, then you. Every one of those generations have to want the best and work for it in everything they do, over and over again is the way I understand it.

"Yous know who wrote-a this-a, Paolo?"

"N-n-n-no," I say. I don't say it could be the Jensens, or maybe some other ignorant kids from school, don't say anything about the rock throwing, either. He'd go to school and stir things up and make it harder for us to catch whoever we got to.

My grandpa Leonardo is short but solid as the trunk of a maple tree. He has a grocery store and a nice house, and when he is driving around town on a Sunday he wears these snappy Italian suits of silk and makes me proud. Right now, he is wearing a white undershirt with little holes in it and tucked in tight to some old suit pants belted high on his stomach. He looks small, and I feel, for the first time, a little afraid for him. I don't want America to hurt him, and the very best way it could hurt him is by disappointing his heart.

But I underestimate him. He hitches up his pants and says, "Paolo, I's a-gonna paint over this-a stuff. It is-a made-a by a fool. They is-a fools in-a any country. This-a nothing. You don-a think on it-a no more." He doesn't even want me to help him. Doesn't want me to look at that sign for any longer than I have already done.

"Well . . . I don't mind . . . not helping," I say.

By the time Billy and I and Georgie take off he is already on a stepladder painting away and humming songs from Italian opera. Italians know opera like Americans know baseball. I watch my grandpa for a bit and think you could beat him with an ax handle made of hickory and he'd just smile at you, his gold eyeteeth winking, and then wrestle you to the ground and still give you a ride home afterward.

"It's Saturday. We have the time, Billy, and we should be mad enough to do something," I say. We are shuffling along down the sidewalk of our block.

He agrees this time, blinking his eyes shut and open with slow, careful thinking. *We need to do one thing first*, he signs.

"Sure."

And tell this to Georgie. Maybe he should learn this. Georgie understands some signing, but not much.

"Okay."

We have to ask Veronica if she thinks it's worth the trouble. Or if we should just stop being friends. I say out loud what he is signing so Georgie knows.

Georgie and I just look at him, our mouths doing our breathing. Even Rufus sits down and starts panting like he's surprised. I think about explaining to Billy about America and our generation, but see he has a point. If Veronica doesn't want to be helping America, we have no business making her. I never thought what could happen to her until now. I nod yes, and we go.

* * *

Where we go is downtown and across the tracks to four blocks of Orange Grove near the corner of Kern and G Streets that Chinese persons like particularly. It starts with Mr. Woo's fish market. We stop there 'cause it is the most interesting store you could see anywhere in the world. I haven't been to anywhere in the world yet, but I have been all around Orange Grove over and over and I have the general idea.

Mr. Woo's got big trays of shaved ice with all kinds of fish laid out there. Mackerels together like they are still swimming in one direction, perches, porgies, and cod, too. Some have big vegetable-heads exploded from coming up from the deep, with hinged jaws hanging open and eyes popped and daring you to just try and eat them.

There are carp still living on the bottoms of leaky barrels. They nudge one another in their sleep down there, not knowing they'll be snagged, then slugged with a wood paddle, wrapped in newspaper, and slapped out in somebody's frying pan before they've even finished up what they were dreaming.

Bunches of lemongrass tied with kite string hang from the awnings, and tables full of pecans, mushrooms, and leeks send up a smell that wakes you complete. Folks are jostling and talking in a kind of up-and-down song that has more treble than bass to it. We are moving around slowly and watching all and almost happy.

Mr. Woo knows my grandpa on account he has a store too. He sees us and waves us round the table of cabbages where he is standing on the crowded sidewalk. He is thin, with a swollen potbelly the size of a bowling ball, and hair slicked down on the sides and bald like Grandpa on the top. "Here," he says. He hands me a paper bag and I look inside and see it is mushrooms, big as footstools. "Your grandfather will appreciate those," he says, and he winks.

I nod.

Georgie asks, "Mr. Woo, can Reds own fish stores?"

I clamp my hands round his mouth and head like its an octopus wanting company. Mr. Woo is looking down at his big, oversize rubber boots, anyway, watching Sammy Woo pouring a bucket of sardines into one corner of them.

Sammy is already graduated from high school, though he never learned a thing. He has fish eyes and ears like big butter-fly wings waving off the sides of his head. He's slow but friendly, and we know him from forever. His dad gets done explaining why he'd rather have the sardines on a table than wriggling in his boots and leaves Sammy to clean up and to talk to us.

"Hey, Sammy," I say.

He looks at me, little flashbulbs of light in his eyes going off—*Pppffftttt!*—then fading. "Fish cost money, Paolo," he says. He's got a sandpaper voice box, and everything he says is raspy.

And he's got some memory of me cheating him, I think, but I have no clue as to why. It's true once I sold him a special pass for a dime to see the moon come up full, but I'd sold those to all the little kids in the neighborhood, not him especially. "We don't want fish, Sammy."

His eyes swim over us slowly. He sees Georgie and Rufus, who he likes. "Hi, Georgie," he says, smiling.

"Hi, Sammy," Georgie answers.

"Did you make your tank costume yet?" Sammy has forgotten about me and Billy completely.

"Nah, Miss Farisi says I have to wait until closer to Halloween."

"You still going to help me figure out my costume?"

"Yep. I was thinking you could go as a giant rabbit?"

Sammy's face drops. "Don't you think that's too scary? I don't want little kids to be scared of Sammy. I was thinking maybe a dragon. Can't I go as a dragon, Georgie?"

"Sure," Georgie says.

"And I can go trick-or-treating with you, right?"

"Yep."

"Hey, guys," I say. "You can figure all this stuff out later. Right now, we need to know where Veronica Cheng lives." You'd think we'd know since Billy has walked her home, but actually she only let him go as far as Mr. Woo's and went the rest on her own.

"Yeah, I could tell you," Sammy says, putting his bucket down and standing up straight.

"Okay, which way?"

"You will need a pass," he says. "Costs a dime."

18.

Who'd a thought Sammy Woo had that amount of clever in him? Just goes to show you can't judge a person's smarts by the grades they get in school. I gave him the dime, and he handed me one sardine. I'd a been mad if I didn't admire him.

I chucked it in the gutter, where Rufus snarfed it up and spit it out, pronto, and we took off to where Sammy told us we could find the Chengs. We come up on the hardware store that her uncle owns and leave Rufus and Georgie to play in the dirt near an old row of privet trees in the alley while we climb the stairs back there to the second story, where there is an apartment they live in. Billy takes a deep breath and knocks.

Luke Cheng opens the door. He's wearing a New York Yankees jersey. "Hey, guys," he says. He doesn't seem surprised nor much impressed that we are there. He looks at Billy and says, "You want Veronica?"

Billy nods.

Luke closes the door.

We wait there, looking round from the little iron porch we are standing on. It's more like a fire escape than anything else. Rufus is down in the alley, curled up, half-asleep, Georgie using him as a pillow. Pretty soon the door opens and Veronica's pretty face peeks out. Her skin is the most fetching you could imagine. Creamy smooth, and then her ink-black bangs and eyes offsetting it. "Billy, you shouldn't have come here," she says, her face clouding.

Billy looks hurt.

"On account of?" I ask.

She looks at me and says, "My father. My father would not like it."

"Because we are Italian?" I ask. "You know Billy ain't Italian. He's full-blooded Appalachian."

Veronica can't help smiling and her eyelashes bat like a shy rare butterfly's wings, and I feel something in my chest go soft. I see how Billy could have such a hankering for her. "No, that's not it." Then she says to Billy, "It's because of my age. And . . . it's because . . . of this town. It . . . it scares my dad. It . . ." She stops talking and just looks at Billy.

That's news, but what strikes me is that I know Billy can read her lips, but how does she know what he says to her? I doubt she knows sign language.

Billy looks at her, soulful, and little shadows of fish slip across the surface of his eyes, and I can tell he wants to know does this mean only that we can't come calling at her house or does this mean she doesn't want to see him at all?

Then I see how they talk, because she's read Billy's thoughts as well as me. "I'll see you at school. But be careful."

I can't help myself and blurt out because I want to be sure, "Billy wants to know if you think you two shouldn't see each other. Even at school. He doesn't want folks to bother you any."

Billy watches me and then looks to Veronica.

She hesitates, and you can tell she is really thinking. Then she says, quickly, "I'll see you at school." Then shuts the door so soft it makes no sound.

We are tramping down the stairs when Luke comes out behind us. He's just a little older than Billy, about the same amount younger to his brothers Matt and Mark as Billy is to me. The last Cheng is John, and he is only four.

"Hey, Paolo," Luke half whispers, half hollers. "Wait!"

We gather halfway down the stairs on a little landing there. "Paolo," he says. "I heard that you guys are tracking Mr. Koski. Is that right?"

I give Billy a look. I haven't told anyone but Hector and eight or nine of my acquaintances at school, but they all crossed their hearts and hoped they would catch some colorful disease that would make their hair fall out and their lips swell, and they're all still looking normal, so I know they kept quiet. I think. But maybe not, because Billy would have had to do some complicated eye-talking to let that slip to Veronica.

Just then Matt and Mark Cheng round the corner coming into the alley. They stop at the bottom of the stairs and look up at us without speaking. You couldn't tell them apart, excepting Mark's face has that rubbly skin a body gets after its had bad acne. They're thin like Luke, have the same thin nose and with that black, black hair like their sister's. They got blue jeans rolled up at the cuff and blue T-shirts, soft from lots of washings. Matt smiles and looks at Mark, then back at us, kind of shy-like. "Hey, Paolo," Matt says. "Billy," he says with a nod.

"Hi," I say.

They come on up the stairs and crowd past us, open their front door to go in. "You coming in, Luke?" Matt says, holding the door, polite, not like my brothers at all.

"Nah, I'm going to show these guys around this part of town."

"Yeah," Matt says. "That's nice. You should." He nods at us all and goes inside.

I'd think them unfriendly except I know them some from elementary school. They were always polite and quiet and were their own best friends. I understand that, since my family hangs with itself pretty much too. Maybe they hang with themselves so people won't give them trouble. I'd never considered that before. I don't see them much in junior high, since we don't share any classes. I know Mark can pitch a fastball quick as a comet and will be going out for baseball same as me come spring.

"So what do you say? Can I help with the tracking?" Luke is whispering.

I'm not saying nothing.

Georgie hollers up to us, "We could use the help. Mr. Koski—"

"Hush up, Georgie," I snap.

Luke looks down at Georgie and then at me and then Billy. He smiles.

"Oh, what the heck. Why exactly is it you're interested?" I ask.

"Things get boring and a little cramped here sometimes, Paolo," he says. "You saw." He swings his arm up toward the front door to the apartment.

Since he wants to throw in with us, I give him a longer, closer look than I have before. He's the same height as Billy, has short, coal black hair that shoots up like bean sprouts, eyes like pecans, and an Adam's apple the size of a peach that bounces up and down when he talks. He's never exactly been our friend but is known as a nice guy at Yosemite Elementary.

He won the science fair there last year building a model volcano that shot some kind of crushed strawberry juice. I remember 'cause we ate most of that lava with our fingers when we visited it in the gymnasium. After what Veronica just said about coming round her house and family, I think maybe I should say no. Yet she's willing to see Billy. "Sure," I say.

19.

"COULD, IF I LET HIM," I ANSWER, MY HEART a fist punching my ribs from the inside and making a few short jabs up toward my throat, making it tough for me to sound hard as I can.

"Shoo-uuut. Shoot!" Edgar says, dragging it out, then spitting it like a bobcat, if bobcats actually spit, that one milky eye of his trying to catch up with its better twin that's focused sharp now and cautious on Rufus. Rufus is straining on his leash out in front of me, not barking or even showing his teeth, but neck-stretched, fur-ruffed, tail pointed straight back, all business and stiff.

"If I was you I wouldn't let it bite me," Edgar says. He's leaning way back, fearful of Rufus yet trying to seem he's not. I notice he's got a loaf of white bread in each hand and no Jeffers. Those loaves aren't in any grocery sack, either, and I don't know why, but I got a definite, quick notion he's just snatched them without paying. Maybe that's 'cause he keeps glancing back toward the screen door of Mary's Corner Home Grocery, where we've just run into one another only an hour after I got home and then sent to the store to get Camel non-filters for Uncle Charlie. Mary is three hundred pounds of pure Hawaiian and the only person who'll sell cigarettes to a kid; she's got ash-sooty skin, rough as rough shingles, the whites of her eyes all swimmy with something runny and yellow as chicken fat. No kid I know would risk lifting even a free tooth-pick off one of her counters.

I mean to say to Edgar that Rufus, who isn't an *it*, won't bite him, except I'm nervous and surprised and can manage to burp out only a low, scratchy, "Ah," that Rufus thinks is his command to go alarmed and crazy. He starts up barking, 'cept he keeps looking back at me, and I think it's plain as day his barking is a happy, I-know-this-game kind of barking. Fortunate for me, Edgar can't tell the difference, 'cause he does a jump-scoot backward that looks like the beginning of some sort of hillbilly dance.

"You keep that thing off me," Edgar says, loud and angry.

I go on and let Rufus keep up his commotion and say right back, feeling bold now, "You keep away from me and Billy, and Rufus will keep off of you."

We hear the screen door squeak on its hinges, and Mary steps out onto the sidewalk not twenty feet from us. I know Edgar sees her too, 'cause he does a fast look back at her before he brings his stare back to Rufus, who is earning the bag of dog food, bunches of carrots, and piles of leftover spaghetti he eats every day. Mary's got on a pink and black tarp of a dress with porpoises and squiggly lines floating all cross it. She folds her arms, swings her wide head, ponytail, and black bangs sideways, spits a worm of tobacco juice neatly into the gutter, then lowers her eyes and examines us.

"That's right," I say. "You mind your own business from now on. All my family and certain persons we're fond of are no longer any concern of yours." Though Rufus has already tired of his game and sat down to watch Mary, her company gives me the burst of the sureness I need.

Then Edgar smiles at me in a way that ain't natural, a smile that's got no bluff or mercy, and the lower parts of my intestines twitch and roll over in their bunks, shuddering like they got a fever. "You and me and Jeffers are going to have a talk by and by about a certain person. You think on that," he says, sneering at Rufus, who has sighed and lain down, just watching with his usual big, soft, I'm-making-less-than-minimum-wage eyes. Then Edgar turns sharp on his heel and moves around and past Mary, going up the block in a hurry as if to meet the dusk that is coming up like dust from the horizon down that way. Mary gives me a study as though I'm something at a yard sale on which she decides she wouldn't care to make an offer.

"Mary," I say, though I've never said anything to her in my life except "One pack of Camels, please" and don't know if she speaks Hawaiian or English or what, so I don't know why I should expect anything of her all of a sudden. "Mary, did you see that?" I ask.

Her mouth is a flat line, and for an answer, she just turns round and steps back into her place, hips swaying like waves, shuddering porpoises left and right.

20.

IT'S ANOTHER WEEK AND A HALF OR MAYBE
two before we get a chance when Luke can meet us. We
decided not to be all that chummy at school so's all that
are minding our business and not their own will leave us be.
We told him to be over at Mrs. Sweeney's garage at three in
the afternoon. We know Mr. Koski doesn't care who Billy
goes with, but he could still want to cause us trouble, since
we caught him with that radio. Besides, we just can't resist
getting an up close look at it. Billy and I and Georgie creep

along Mrs. Sweeney's driveway. We promised Luke we'd wait there on him by the garage and not go in without him. We didn't need to promise. Someone's put a shiny brass dead-bolt lock on that garage. It's on the bottom of the sliding wooden door, and whoever did the job took the time to drill a hole in the cement down there so the bolt could drop in secure.

Luke slips up behind us while we are looking at it. "Hey, Georgie. Billy. Paolo. Rufus," he whispers, nodding to each of us in turn.

We nod back.

"Sledgehammer?" I say.

Billy shakes his head violent-like.

Luke looks uncomfortable.

Georgie just squints.

I look him over carefully. "Georgie," I say. "Suppose I was to boost you up. Do you think you could get in that little window out back of the garage?"

"Sure." He takes right off running, happy as Georgie gets.

We follow. Back of the place, in a two-foot-wide space between the fence and the wall of the garage, is a little window, cobwebbed, dirt-caked, but big enough for Georgie to get through. We all scoot up to it. I give it a try. It doesn't budge. But I can tell it's not locked, just stuck. We all scrunch in there together, Billy and Luke and me, and push up on it. It complains some but gives way in short, sharp jerks until it's all the way up.

I stoop down and Georgie gets on me piggy-back, then climbs up onto my shoulders. I bust sweat standing us up, my legs wobbly. "Be careful," I tell him before I stumble forward and he flies off through the window. We all stand there waiting to hear if he's all right. We don't hear a thing. We look at one another. If Georgie's in there neck-broke and dead, we have explaining to do. We will end up on the front page of the paper. I'm wondering what shirt I should wear for the photo when we see Georgie. He's got his head stuck out the window, looking down on us.

"I'm this tall because I'm standing on a table, Paolo."

"That's fine, Georgie," I say.

"There's rat poop in here."

"Okay," I say.

"No rats, though," he says.

"Georgie, will you go throw the bolt open on the door in front?"

"I already did."

"Well, why didn't you say so?"

"Because I locked it back again."

"What?"

"Had to," he says.

"Whatever for, Georgie?"

"Mr. Koski's Dodge truck pulled up the driveway when I was just peeking out."

"Holy moly."

"And Paolo, Mr. Koski was in it."

We are frozen for a second. Then we move fast. Georgie jumps and I crash-land-catch him. It'd be nice to listen through the window, but Mr. Koski would know it was open. He'll notice it anyway, since we don't have time to shut it. We just run around the side of the garage and peek. See the front door just now sliding closed behind him as he goes in.

"That was close," Luke says. He looks flushed, excited. I think he might be our kind of guy, one that likes to go wilding. We are going down the driveway and can't resist giving that Dodge panel truck a looking-over. We leave our face prints smudged on the driver's-side window.

"What's he got in the back of this truck?" Georgie asks.

We go round there. A panel truck is a little like a station wagon, with no windows except in the front and the back like a funeral wagon. Standing on the rear bumper and looking through the windows we can't see a thing, so I try the door handle and it opens. We all pile in. There's scads of room back there and some cardboard boxes stacked up behind the driver's seat. Luke closes the door so we can get the full feel of it, just as Rufus starts barking from out in the drive. When Mr. Koski comes out and climbs in and starts it and we hunker down behind those boxes, it is Rufus he watches so he won't run him over as he pulls away.

21.

MR. KOSKI SINGS WHILE HE DRIVES. Sings, *"If I had a hammer, I'd hammer in the morning, I'd hammer in the evening, ah-all over this land. I'd hammer out free-e-dom, I'd hammer out ju-us-stice, I'd hammer out love and . . ."* and so on and on as we go shooting across Orange Grove and out into the country. I never knew a teacher could be such a happy sort on his downtime.

We can tell where we are in a fashion, 'cause lying on our backs we can see tops of buildings and telephone poles and trees and sky flashing by in the back window. It takes no more than five minutes to be in the country on account Orange Grove is so small. But Mr. Koski keeps driving for maybe twenty minutes or so before he pulls off the avenue he's on and starts bumping us down a dirt road.

I'm thinking if he catches us—and he is going to catch us if he gets into those boxes—he could bury us out here and no one would be the wiser unless there was a hard rain, and we floated up on some rancher's porch, and that wouldn't do us any good since we'd be all the way dead by then.

Maybe Billy and I and Luke could tackle him and Georgie could get away. He can run fast as a cat. Actually, he prefers running to walking. Going to school every day, he'll like as not run ahead a block and then back to Billy and me the whole time we are going. I realize it won't really help us since the rest of us would still get planted.

The Dodge hiccups to a stop, a cloud of dust rolling past the windows. Mr. Koski shifts into park, swivels round in his seat, smiles with teeth flashing like Franklin Delano Roosevelt used to in newsreels, knocks his head back, and says, "The ride isn't free, boys. You'll have to help."

22.

HELPING IS GOING UP AND DOWN ROWS OF
alfalfa and checking to see if there are any rats in little cage-
traps Mr. Koski has set all heck and gone over everywhere. He
catches those rats and weighs them, minus the weight of the
cage, checks the numbers they have on these little tin wrist-
bands he's given them, and then lets 'em go. It's science.

Myself, I could tell without running a rat prison that they
would get fat living in a neighborhood of alfalfa and a thousand other things folks grow. But the science of biology isn't

any fun without the tramping round in the fields and woods, I suppose. Mr. Koski is happy as Georgie stomping all over the place, eyes lighting up when he finds one of his cages with a customer in it.

He didn't say a thing about what we were doing in his truck or anything else. Just that he appreciated the volunteer help, and then he laughed. If Mr. Koski didn't wear a dirty felt Montana hat, he'd look exactly like Santa Claus probably did when he was younger. He doesn't seem a bad sort at all, but Communists probably have all kinds of ways to get you to go over to their side.

"Mr. Koski," Georgie says when we are all gathered round, just about finished with that big field and looking at the last trap with two rats in it, which Mr. Koski says are a Mr. and Mrs. "Why don't you just catch the rats in Mrs. Sweeney's garage?"

His eyes do that twinkling a teacher's eyes do when you've screwed up and asked them just the very thing they'd love to talk to you about for half an hour or more, until your ears go blind or you have to practice sleeping with your eyes open, which I have very nearly mastered once Ernie showed me how.

"These are not just any rodents. These are special. Not very many of them left. They are found only in this valley and in the foothills around here. San Joaquin Valley kangaroo rat.

See how they have only four toes on their hind feet instead of five?"

How many are there? Are they worth money? Do the farmers poison them? Would a crow eat a special rat? Does a rat know it's a rat? What would a rat taste like if you cooked it in batter like a french fry? Mr. Koski answers all of Georgie's questions, even the last, and I don't really hear a word he says 'cause I'm just watching his lips as he talks and thinking he is way too crazy to be a harm to anyone, even if he is a Communist.

* * *

Since he's got no plan to bury us, Mr. Koski wants us home in time for supper, so we take off directly. Georgie sits in the passenger seat and the rest of us crowd up close behind him.

"Sir," I say. Say sir to a grown-up and they will fall all over themselves to help you out. If you don't believe it, just try it out. "Sir, what kind of name is Koski?"

"Kind?" he says.

"What brand of country?"

"Oh, Finnish."

He doesn't mean finish what I am asking, he means his people are from Finland. Ernie told me that Finlanders are the most depressed of all the peoples of the world. Says they sit in the dark all winter and cry and sometimes they go into a sauna and whip themselves with juniper branches to keep themselves awake and grateful. Mr. Koski could definitely be lying, since he is not depressed in the littlest bit.

"How far can a ham radio set get a signal?" I slip that in while Mr. Koski is thinking about Finland.

I see his blue eyes smiling in the rearview mirror. "It depends on the antenna. Mine will reach the foothills. Fifteen miles."

"Is Russia more than fifteen miles from Mrs. Sweeney's garage?" Georgie asks.

Mr. Koski looks over at him. Georgie is looking straight ahead and picking his nose and seems more interested in what he might dig out than in the answer to his question.

"Yes, that's a bit farther than my signal goes. Boys," he says, "I was a radio operator in the service, and I've always had an interest in radios. I talk to a couple of fellows around here who have sets and who share my interest in the animals of the valley."

"Why don't you just use the telephone?" Georgie says.

"Well . . . it's just more fun this way, I guess."

And I flat believe him. I am surprised, but I've been surprised before. I believe him 'cause I know him some now. I already knew the fanciest of imagining about folks is nothing compared to knowing them direct. But I'm surprised, and I am surprised that I am glad, and that my glad is genuine. I see, too, that grown-ups like to do things just for the heck of it, like using a ham radio instead of telephone, the same as any kid. Makes me consider the hard fact that I might not have any good reason to put off growing up anymore.

23.

GEORGIE IS GOING TRICK-OR-TREATING AS a paper-mâché tank. It's too big an idea and so too big of a costume, but Georgie isn't having any of my advice on the subject. Sammy will probably be a dragon. Says his dad already has a red and black one wired together out of sticks and paper and muslin, sort of the way a kite is made. It's left over from Chinese New Year's. Billy and I are going as World War I troops and Luke says he will possibly be a cotton plant.

"Cotton plant?" I ask. We are loafing around out back of

our place the next day, which is Saturday, where our tree house used to be.

"My brothers and I picked cotton last summer. We had to get up really early every morning and drive out to Tulare with my dad and pick cotton for J. D. Leswell and Company."

"So what?" Picking stuff that grows is no big deal in Orange Grove.

"Well, I kept a bunch of cotton branches to remember by, to remember not to grow up and have to do that kind of work." He looks at me as if that explains everything, then goes on, "I thought I could wrap them around me with masking tape and have a costume no one else has."

"Or ever will." Then I catch myself and don't say more. No use discouraging a person about his ideas. Lots of times the only thing they got is their ideas and in that case, a nutty one will do just fine. Billy is jabbing a penknife that Uncle Charlie gave him a long time ago into the black bark of what is left of our tree. He's got a faraway look, and I know he wishes he could hang with Veronica on a Saturday. That's why I got everybody together— to cheer him up and get our minds on fixing our costumes.

Rufus comes up to us. Georgie is trailing him, covered in soot and ashes and looking like a gingerbread man with eyes made out of white chocolate. "We can go over to Miss Farisi's," he says.

Not a bad idea, not a bad idea at all, I think; even Billy perks up at the thought of it. But I say, "Aren't you supposed to wait until just before Halloween to get her to make your tank?"

"We can go today, Paolo. She said so. It's only two more weeks. Or a week and a half. Well, it's on a Wednesday."

That gives me a bit of a shock. I've been thinking about all that's been happening to us and lost track. We haven't even set for sure what we are doing at the carnival after we do our trick-or-treating. Gosh almighty. Tomorrow Billy and I will serve Mass; we are going to have to talk to Monsignor about it. And it's about time we talked to him about some other stuff too. Time has got away from me like is its nature I know, but it rattles me. "Let's go," I say. We take off directly, single file, across the burnt field like we're on safari, Georgie and Rufus ranging out in front and looping back in big, lazy eights.

We are coming up on the Sun-Maid raisin packing plant, a red brick place big as three cathedrals out in a field of knee-high yellow grass and right next to the railroad tracks. Has a dirt parking lot with a slew of cars, most of them with gray primered fenders or cracked windshields or dimples in their bumpers. They are here even on a Saturday, since this is when raisins come out of the miles and miles of vines that we have all round Orange Grove.

Even Grandpa and Grandma Leonardo worked in the fields

when they first got to California. After awhile Grandpa moved up to the packing houses and was even in charge of one before he got his grocery store going. Like Luke, we are supposed to finish school so's not to grow up with a permanent crick in our back from bending the way pickers do. It's honest work, but it's hard, they say.

We are slipping round the far side of the parking lot, short-cutting to the edge of it, where the south side of town starts and where Miss Farisi has her little house, when the rear door to a brown DeSoto four-door sedan swings open, blocking our way. Edgar Jensen piles out, Jeffers Jensen falling out after him. They both stand up. I forgot that their mom works gluing labels to wooden Sun-Maid boxes. They must have gone to work with her, for what reason I don't know, and have been sleeping in the car this morning. I can tell since their eyes, both of them, are blurry, tiny teaspoons of sleep goop in the corners.

Rufus and Georgie are out front of us by three hundred yards, so Billy and Luke and I just stand there and see what is going to be what. I never told Billy about my running into Edgar in front of Mary's. Figured he had enough worry on his mind. Truth is the Jensens look as surprised as we are. I see Edgar trying to think, thoughts twitching and twisting up from his mouth to his eyebrows and back.

"Hey, Edgar," I say. "Hey, Jeffers."

"Hey, yourself," Jeffers says, then looking up at his brother.

Three of us facing two of them, but Edgar is two years older than me and has arms strong as bridge cables and a hill person's way of fighting, which is don't fight or else do—fight to hurt the one you are sore at to the point he'll not ever look your way again. Town boys will fight right in front of a teacher, 'cause they know the teacher will break it up even if that teacher gets his glasses broke doing it. A hill boy fights like he hunts— 'cause he needs to, not for sport. I notice they don't have their boots on. I got the cheap pair of boots Grandma Leonardo gave me last Christmas, but me and my boots couldn't take the Jensens even if they are standing there in their socks. Maybe they are going to get waked up and fight us fair and square, out in the open, instead of all their terrorizing and burning and graffiti, if they are the ones who've been doin' it. I look off and see Rufus gone ahead with Georgie, and I hope this isn't the time we got to wrassle 'em, 'cause we'll lose. I replay some of my sister's pit bull wrestling moves in my head in case, stretch my jaw, and get ready.

And then Billy takes a half step forward and signs, *Halloween is almost here. What are you guys' costumes going to be?* Billy has guts.

They have no knowledge of what he's signed, so I say it.

They look like somebody kicked them. Maybe embarrassed. Luke says, "I'm going to be a cotton plant."

That leaves them more puzzled than they already are. They already think we are as stupid as town boys could be. They look at Luke as if he's lost his mind, hanging round with us and on top of that wanting to be a cotton plant.

"Georgie is going as a tank and Rufus is going to be an *attack* dog."

Edgar just squints, once, at me for saying that.

"You guys have Halloween in the hills where you came from?" I know they were not in Orange Grove last October. They look at each other again. I get the feeling they are best-friends brothers, the kind that fight all the time but look after each other just as fierce.

"How come you are sleeping in your mom's car?" I can't help asking.

Jeffers says, kind of blurting, "Our dad run off. We got to live in it now." Edgar grabs his younger brother's elbow to pinch him quiet, but Jeffers shakes him off, steps sideways, seems to need to get things off his chest. "We wash in the restroom at Roeding Park. Eating mostly fruit we pick."

I bet they have never done Halloween, Billy signs to me, his eyes thoughtful.

I don't translate that and Edgar takes it as an insult, I guess, 'cause he says, the little gears in his voice box meshing harsh, "You three git, now. Go on. Today ain't the day we got anything to say to you." He's as mad at his brother as he is at us. "Go on, git!"

He means it, and I'm happy to grab hold of Billy and walk backward and then around the car on the other side and off. I notice the inside of that car is trashed up good, with mashed papers and blankets and one logging boot laid on its side, up on the dashboard. We had no intention of shaming them, but if Edgar being embarrassed is what's kept him from snapping our necks, I'm not arguing.

We are on past the parking lot when Rufus and Georgie come panting up to us. "Paolo," Georgie says, huffing, "Veronica is at Miss Farisi's!"

24.

"Okay, sweetheart," Miss Farisi says to Georgie, winding her tape measure back around her hand, "you can step down." Of course, he about faints off that table, going limp, me having to help him to stand. Can't say a thing he's so bug-eyed in love with his teacher. She doesn't seem to notice or else is used to everyone half-mad for her. She hasn't even scolded him for being all ash-sooty.

We are in her kitchen, sitting round a table with a red and white checkered Italian tablecloth. Billy is sitting across from

Veronica just looking at her, Luke is sort of watching the both of them, and I'm standing, holding Georgie up, but mostly watching Miss Farisi. She reminds me of a doe I saw one morning in a cornfield stepping high and dainty, nuzzling dew and sunlight from those stalks. Once it saw me it looked at me with its eyes the size of ripe avocados for one long moment, and then it just floated away, legs of smoke, gone. But Miss Farisi is all of her standing there in her loose white blouse and her dungarees and little red canvas shoes and is letting us get as much of her close up as our eyes can hold.

"Okay, boys, can you get that chicken wire I have on the back porch?" she says. Luke and I and Georgie scramble out of there like we are doing a fire drill, smashing one another in the doorway and snatching that roll and fighting to haul it in. Billy doesn't move.

Miss Farisi lifts Georgie back onto the table and starts mashing that chicken wire in all manner of directions, making a cannon of some of it to stick off the square part of it that is supposed to be the tank body part. She has the tip of her tongue bit in her teeth and tiny beads of perspiration forming above her lip. She leaves a slit in the back of the contraption so's he can climb in and out of it once it's all done.

She works; we watch. She says, "Isn't it nice that Veronica came by, boys?"

Sure, we all nod. Who knew they were friends?

"Of course, now you're here, there won't be any more girl talk."

Veronica drops her eyes.

Billy's eyes go down too.

Luke watches them. He looks like he feels sorry for them.

"Miss Farisi," Georgie says, kind of stunned, what with being so close to her. "Once we get the plaster of Paris on this . . . can we paint it?"

"I certainly would say so. Green. And we'll put a white American star on it too." She smiles at him.

That sends him wobbling round the moon once or twice. I get ready to catch him if he decides to come out of orbit in my direction.

Rufus, who is in the kitchen with us 'cause Miss Farisi is the only adult nice enough to let him come indoors, comes up behind her and sniffs her lavender perfume and then lays himself down, looking up at her, tail thumping the floor.

"Veronica," I think to say, polite, "have you got your costume yet?"

She looks at me. Eyes like night sky with little stars.

Luke speaks for her. "We don't have Halloween. I'm going 'cause you guys are. Sammy Woo goes because he's more American than Chinese."

"Yeah, but Monsignor made the carnival for everybody," I say.

"He made it Chinese Lantern Night since it already was that. We don't have to do trick-or-treating."

"Who'd miss out on that?" I say.

The Jensens, Billy signs like he's trying to tell me it's okay if American-Chinese persons aren't the only ones that might not go trick-or-treating.

Miss Farisi looks at me with her eyebrows raised Mrs. Ogilbee-style, so I know I'm to translate and tell about the Jensens, how we don't think they do Halloween on account they probably can't afford costumes, so I do.

"I think those boys have more worries right now than Halloween," she answers to that, concern in her voice. She and Veronica give a quick look at each other, and I wonder what all they've been talking about.

"You know the Jensens, Miss Farisi?" I ask. "I mean to talk to?"

"They aren't two who are much for talking," she says, her attention back on arranging Georgie in his chicken wire. She has one of her arms in there up to its elbow, sort of stuffing him this way and that, getting the shape of the thing proper and tight. "Maybe it's for the best they aren't going, since you don't get along, anyway." Her lips are mashed thin with concentrating.

My head snaps round at that, over to Billy, back up to Miss

Farisi. "You know anything about Edgar and Jeffers we ought to know?" It comes out of me honest and without my thinking, and I see Miss Farisi is a person maybe I trust. We all trust. It occurs to me how all of us are there in her kitchen like family, and I think she is going to be a number one Italian-American mom to somebody someday.

"Well," she says, "I know Jeffers Jensen has an awful crush on Veronica." She lets that sink in some, not looking at anyone or anything except Georgie's cage. "Honestly, he came by my room to ask more questions about girls than he probably has asked about anything in his entire life."

My mouth is dry and drops open as slow as if it's chock-full of peanut butter. Veronica blushes. Billy looks at me as if to be sure he's understood the lips of what Miss Farisi's saying and I nod, *Yes*, slow, back at him.

"I realize a teacher doesn't go around telling what a student confides in her, but I am doing just that and for a reason. I feel there is a danger for you boys, and I mean all of you, including Jeffers and Edgar. You could get hurt if you all don't put a stop to this nonsense. I didn't like the anger in Jeffers's voice when he spoke to me, and I told him so. Told him when one is hurt by love it doesn't give you the right to hurt anyone else." She pulls her arm out of Georgie's tank skeleton and lays her eyes on me. "Has anyone been hurt?"

I manage to close up my mouth and answer right back out of habit, I guess, like she is a teacher again, not anyone's Italian mom. "Nobody's been hurt."

"Well . . . that's what Veronica says too." Miss Farisi has some smart-aleck in her voice I never heard before.

Veronica isn't looking at anyone. My mind has started to trot hard and is about to break into a gallop. Is this why the Jensens have been dogging us? I thought they had a problem with Veronica being with Billy 'cause she was Chinese. That don't make sense if Jeffers wants to be Billy and have his girl sweet on himself. Does Miss Farisi know how much has been going on? If she did, she'd be more than just irritated. Does . . .

"Hey!" Georgie hops sideways on the table. "Ouch!"

"Oh, dear, I'm sorry," says Miss Farisi. It looks as if Georgie's got stuck in the butt with some pointy bit of chicken wire. He's grabbing his cheeks back there. She turns him round to inspect on the area closely, then just yanks his pants and his underpants down in one motion, pushes round with her thumbs, yanks his pants and all back up in one motion, and says, "No blood. No damage. Sorry, kiddo, I am not paying attention to what I am doing."

Georgie is frozen stuck, can't speak or move, except for his eyes that are pointed at the ceiling, tracing back and forth in an arc. It's just more than his brain can process. The whole room is quiet except for Miss Farisi bending chicken wire. Nobody says anything. Then, to rescue him maybe, Miss Farisi asks, "And . . . and so what exactly is Chinese Lantern Night, Luke?"

Still no one speaks. Miss Farisi whips her head around at us and cocks her head, quizzical.

That's when Veronica's voice comes, soft, "It's a very old tradition," she says.

Luke flicks his eyes over to her, opens his mouth to speak, thinks otherwise. Lets her tell it.

We all look at her. She has her head still partly down and seems to be talking to the table. "The Chinese from around here come from a province that has always celebrated it."

"What're they celebrating?" I ask, my mind needing the story, needing its distraction, needing time to understand all I've learned and am learning, if that's what is happening.

"Well, not really a celebration," Luke says.

"More of a commemoration," Veronica says.

"Commemoratin' what?" I ask, almost listening.

"Long ago there were two . . . two lovers."

Billy's head goes up, slow.

"Everybody in the town said they didn't belong together because the boy had come from another village. But the two didn't see it that way. They wanted to marry. Everyone was against it and did many things to stop them seeing each other. But they went on."

"How come everyone was so dead against them?" I ask, curious now.

"I don't know. It's a very old story."

"So what's that got to do with lanterns?"

"Well, the two, the two . . . were heartbroken that they couldn't be together, and one day they went to the sea and stood on a cliff and vowed they could not suffer being apart."

She stops. Miss Farisi stops her work. Everyone listens.

"They held hands and then . . . jumped." Veronica is looking up now and out of Miss Farisi's kitchen window. It's gotten late and the dusk is swimming around out there. "As they fell toward the sea something wonderful happened: They turned into cranes . . . and they flew away." Her voice drops away like the beating of wings. "Flew away together."

"Where did they fly to?" Georgie says, all caged and monkey-curious and believing the whole story.

"That's an awfully grown-up tale, Veronica," Miss Farisi says, thoughtful.

"Yeah, and kinda mushy, too, but where do the lanterns figure in?" I ask.

"Well, ever after, on the evening when it happened, the townspeople would make paper lanterns in the shapes of birds, put tiny candles inside them, and set them afloat on the water."

"Huh?"

"There's no ocean around here. Chinese just hang a lantern outside their door," Luke says.

"Not . . . not a very happy story," I say. Though I admit I kind of liked the flying-away part.

"Are you coming with Sammy to the carnival?" Georgie asks Veronica from inside his chicken coop.

"I may be. Or I may be over in Reedley with my grandmother."

"Why's that, Veronica?" asks Miss Farisi.

"No special reason."

"Oh, that's too bad. I thought you might go to the carnival with me."

"Grandma is getting old and needs the help," Luke explains.

"Well, let me know," Miss Farisi says.

"Is it too late for us to make this tank into a bird?" Georgie says. He's been taken with the story.

"Yes, little mister, it certainly is," she says. Then she pokes his rib with her finger through the wire.

He blushes, dark as plums, dumb and blind.

I'm thinking about those Chinese lovebirds. I know no Italian would jump off a cliff for love. They might go to singing and howling and draping themselves around on the furniture, but they ain't going to actually jump off of or out of anything. I have enough Italian aunts to know that. In fact, when Aunt Genevieve wouldn't marry Jimmy DiJemmo on account he quit his job at the butcher shop so's to be a saxophone player, he came round the house with a razor threatening to cut his own throat, but after a lot of commotion he left in time to make it home for his mom's dinner and never came back.

But I ain't the one in love. I look at Billy. He looks okay. And he's 100 percent Appalachian. There is no way *ever* an Appalachian gets excited like that. I still remember when I was little, listening to my dad and my uncle and my grandpa on that side, who's passed on, sitting out on a summer evening, having conversations:

"Nice out."

Five minutes with nobody saying a thing.

"Yep."

Five more minutes.

"Cooling some."

Five more minutes while I am going out of my mind and getting itchy all over, while they're not twitching one tiny muscle.

"Heard the neighbor woman died."

Five more minutes.

"Hmm."

Five minutes.

"Say it was on account the water round here is poison."

Five more.

"Hmm."

Ten minutes.

"You want some of that iced tea now?"

And so on. I have no worries 'bout Billy whatsoever. Well, I don't think I do. Maybe I do. He already is only one of maybe six fifth graders I know that has a girlfriend he hangs with. His mom doesn't care much for him and leaves him to live with us, so who is it that really knows?

Well, Georgie is all done up in chicken wire tank-fashion like he wanted, and Miss Farisi helps him slip out of it. We been there so long it's almost all the way dark.

Miss Farisi takes Georgie's "tank" into another room and comes back to find us all at the table waiting on her next plan for us.

She smiles and looks at us and then at me, I suppose since I'm the oldest, looks at me with a little cat-eye twinkle and a sigh, says, "Well, I suppose since it is getting dark, I could drive you home."

"Oh . . . well, no, that's okay. We pretty much walk everywhere."

"We don't have to leave yet," Georgie says.

"It's only a five-minute walk," I say.

Luke stands up. "It's time I take Veronica home. My dad is going to be wondering about us. About Veronica."

Veronica looks at him like she's happy he's her brother and looking out for her, and also like the mention of her father has awakened her, as if she's been sleeping and dreaming. I realize she and Luke look a lot alike. She stands up quickly, and Billy, too. The two glance at each other, something passing between them like a quick, dark bird darting from one bush to another, so fast you aren't sure you actually saw it.

"I would rather not travel on an empty stomach," Georgie says. He hasn't budged an inch.

"Well, Georgie, it so happens I have a date tonight, and I will be going out to dinner."

All of us swing our heads toward her. A teacher? A date? With a *man*?

Georgie looks like he's just ate the tablecloth and is having trouble digesting it, mumbling something to himself and coughing.

I swear none of us can move after that. Miss Farisi is trying to get her mind around what is the matter with us. Then she perks up with an idea and says, "I tell you what, how would you like to take a peek at Saturn, and then I'll have to let you leave?"

Just because you are beautiful doesn't mean you can't have

a mind. Not that you'd need one if you looked like Miss Farisi, but apparently she's got one anyway. She takes us through the house, on through her bedroom, done up all frills and pillows and bows and all the typical dust-catching, fire-hazard girly stuff and then out through some French doors to a patio made of red tile. There she's got a good-sized professional-looking telescope. We crowd right round it, and she shows us how to look into this little spot and there, bright and clear as in one of Mrs. Sweeney's books, is Saturn, rings and all.

While everyone is looking, I notice that John Muir Junior High is stenciled on the tripod of that telescope, and I know then it is Mr. Edmund's telescope, and he is the one probably going to dinner with her. But all I can say when I look again is, "Gosh, it looks just like Saturn."

"That's because it is, silly," she says, her perfume and her eyes and her cheek close to mine.

Truth is, that night I lie in bed a long time thinking about Jeffers, about Billy and even Veronica's sky-black eyes. I lie there smelling Miss Farisi's perfume and thinking of her eyes like warm dark chocolate, and imagining Mr. Edmund, who will most likely marry her someday, the two of them just loafing around, looking at the planets whenever they want. I fall asleep awful and slow, awful with some kind of silly, dreaming of all those heavenly bodies that aren't mine.

25.

HECTOR SNAPS A TOWEL ACROSS THE TIP OF my nose. "Dad wants to know why he got a bill for the paper, hotshot."

That ends my dreaming lickety-split. I forgot I signed him up for the paper, him thinking we got it for free. I sit up and look at my alarm clock. Nine thirty a.m. Billy and I are supposed to serve Mass at ten o'clock! Hector is already gone from my room, not much interested in my doings. I shake Billy out. Georgie is already up and gone somewheres.

We hustle down R Street to Mariposa where the Cathedral
of San Joaquin stands, biggest building in Orange Grove excepting the courthouse. We go in round the back, get our altar boy
costumes on, get onstage and light up the candles like a hundred
birthdays and are ready when Monsignor sweeps in. Monsignor
does Mass in a jiffy. He's good at it. Swings the long sleeves of
his vestments round with authority and style, belting out Latin
and genuflecting and marching snappy as any Marine.

He's done in thirty-five minutes and is pulling his gear off
when Billy and I corner him in his dressing room. "What . . .
what is it, boys?" he asks, backing up, when he sees us creeping
up on him.

"We wanted to ask about us having a special booth at the
carnival."

Billy nods at me and then Monsignor.

"A psychic fortune booth," I say. We know we don't have any
information on folks, but we figure it's still a good idea. We
could just make stuff up on the spot.

Monsignor smiles, crooked. He disappears inside his getup,
pulling some of it over his head, pops out again, face red, strug-
gling like he's personally mad at his clothes for giving him a fight.
Eventually he gets the thing off and laid out on a table. Turns to
us. "Well, I already have you two signed up for a very important
job." Monsignor is bald-head Irish and mostly friendly.

"Important?" I say.

"That's right, Paolo. Besides, all that fortune-telling stuff isn't exactly the way of the church."

"No?"

"I'm afraid that is the work of our main competitor."

"Sears and Roebuck?" I'm thinking of the ads in the catalogue for women's slips and the gear they wear under dresses.

"What?" Monsignor says. "Paolo, I am talking about the dark one of all history."

"Ernie?"

Now Monsignor is getting frustrated.

"Madam Sophie?"

Nose flushing up, eyes crossing.

Billy signs to me, *The devil, dummy.*

I'm thinking of the strangeness of Billy calling me a dummy when Monsignor barks, "Roving cleanup crew. You two will walk around with a trash can and pick up messes when you spot them!" He half shouts it over his shoulder as he sweeps out of the room.

We chase after him and catch up to him on the sidewalk.

"That's it, boys. It's not negotiable." He keeps walking.

"No, Monsignor, it's not that. We wanted to ask about another thing."

He stops, snaps his wristwatch up, pushed far away from

his eyes. We know he's got to go to dinner with the Bianchis or some other family as usual.

"Monsignor," I say, quick as I can, "if someone or more than one was trying to keep you from seeing a certain someone on account they liked that someone, would it be okay to sic your dog on 'em? Just enough so's they stop?"

"What?"

"If a deaf kid liked a Chinese girl and some hillbillies were upset and terrorizing those two over it, would it be okay to catch them alone, sleeping or something? Maybe tie them up and beat on them enough so's they'd quit?" I gotta be crazy. I didn't mean to put it to him in that way at all, but Monsignor being in a rush threw me.

Now we have his full attention. He stands up straight and closes his eyes. Opens them and looks at me, then Billy. Each glance a drill cranked hard. I notice Billy looks as if he could smack me. Monsignor notices too, then looks up, eyeballs scanning the distance. Then slowly he comes back to us, says, "If it was the Jensen boys that was bothering me, I'd think it smart to steer clear of them."

"But Monsignor, don't you got to fight the devil?"

Monsignor lifts his eyebrows.

"Jesus whipped on the moneychangers," I say, sort of weak, but getting it out there.

"*You* are not Jesus." He lets that sink in, his eyes bright as lit ends of cigars. They cool some and he says, "Oh, Paolo, I'm not even talking about right, I mean I am, but I'm talking about smart, too. Those two things can be the same thing sometimes. The Jensen boys aren't the devil. They . . . well, I'll . . . speak to their mother. But you two would do better to take care and keep track of the devil in yourselves."

"In ourselves? Monsignor, I put Satan behind me. Long time ago. Billy, too."

Billy nods, genuine, concerned.

Monsignor frowns, then gets that leprechaun smile he can get, leans down to us close, whispers, "Well, he's caught up to you; breathing on your necks right now."

26.

THAT'S THE TROUBLE WITH BEING A CHURCH-goer. Can ruin three-fourths of your plans and ambitions. On top of everything else, Billy and I will be walking around half out of our wits every time we hear a leaf scratching the sidewalk behind us, whipping round all the time something foolish, looking out for Satan.

On the other hand, being cleanup crew isn't really that big of a blow. We'll still have our Halloween and costumes and carnival. I realize I'd known for a while that Billy had been right—we probably wouldn't be doing a booth, anyway. And too much else has been going on that needed our attention. And still does.

We're home now, and already I've lost track of Georgie and Billy, thinking on things like I am. I got lots to do, figuring about how to deal with whomever it is is our problem. And also how to make Arthur Sweeney's gear into two soldier's costumes for me and Billy. We have exactly ten days till Halloween.

Maria-Teresina-the-Little-Rose drifts past me, saying, "Dad's up in his room, and I'm supposed to tell you to go talk to him if I ever get a chance to lay eyes on you, and I have." I do a double take. Maria-Teresina-the-Little-Rose is four years old and two feet tall and has a habit of repeating what's she's been told as near to word for word so's she doesn't get it wrong. She's just old enough to take pride in it. Anyway, I don't need Dad on my case right now, so I jet up the stairs going Mach 2, which I am not supposed to do ever, and catch Georgie at the landing, there at the halfway point. He's scooting down the stairs and gets my legs tangled up and we go rolling and bumping all the way down.

"Dang it, Georgie. Where you going in such a hurry?"

He's lying facedown, arms out like he fell from a plane with no parachute. "I was looking for you," he says, soft, to the floor.

"What for?" I say, sitting up, rubbing my neck.

"To give you this." He has a bit of crumpled paper in the hand of one of his outstretched arms.

I reach over and take it. Unfold it. It's a note. In code. In a girl's handwriting.

"Where'd you get this, Georgie?" I ask slowly.

"In the little drawer of me and Billy's nightstand." He's still talking weak, facedown to the hardwood floor.

"I've got to decode this."

"I already did."

"Really?" I say.

"Says, 'I can't see you anymore.'"

"Ohhhhhh boy, Billy's not going to like that one bit. Georgie, we got to find him. Right now," I say, sitting up.

"Paolo?"

"Yeah?"

"You mind if I just rest here a bit?"

"It's a bit early for a nap, Georgie. Besides, folks are likely to walk on you, lying in the way like that."

"Ooooohhh," he groans. He knows it's my fault he fell, and I'm in trouble if anyone finds out.

"I can put a caution sign on you if you like," I say. "But that's no guarantee someone won't step on your head and crunch it like a melon."

He turns his head toward me, looks at my boots, and frowns.

We both know he's all right. He smiles. He's learning.

I jump up and slip upstairs and next thing I know I'm in my dad's room doing the last thing I would choose to be doing, explaining that newspaper subscription.

"It was a promotion," I say.

"So why the charge of a dollar ninety-five?" he asks.

"First month free. If you want to keep it after, they charge."

"We've only received the paper for a month."

"Right, a dollar ninety-five for a month."

"No. It's free for the first month."

"Yeah, that's what I was saying."

"I've got a bill here charging me for one month."

"This month?"

"Last month."

"Last month was the promotion, and this month you got to pay the dollar ninety-five."

"Son." My dad is getting sore now but keeping his temper, since he knows I get lousy grades in math. "There should be no charge."

"Exactly," I say, nodding.

"But there is a charge."

I take a deep breath. "That's the nonpromotional charge."

My dad's ears are so full of blood they're jam-red and pulsing. "All right, mister," he says in a whisper, "you come up with a nonpromotional one dollar and ninety-five cents, pay these people, *and* you cancel the paper."

"Sure, Dad. No problem." I leave it at that and dart out of that room.

"Paolo." My dad doesn't even raise his voice. Knows I'd be listening. Knows I didn't think I'd get out of there that easy.

"Yeah, Dad?" I lean my head back into the doorway.

"You got a minute?"

He knows he owns all the minutes I got or will get until I am eighteen and buying my own groceries. "Sure," I say, generous-like and helpful, as always.

"You don't mind sitting down, do you?" He motions to the little nightstand chair.

"No, I don't mind." I sit. He's got more on his mind than that dollar ninety-five.

He's got his back to me, fiddling with his watch and cuff links and stuff on the top of his dresser. "You know if you ever were to get into some fix that you couldn't find a way out of, you would come to me." It's not a question.

"Yes, sir."

"Jack Branigan told me that fire was very likely an accident of some kind."

"Jack?"

"Captain Jack."

"Oh, right, fire chief. Captain Jack."

He makes a very faint snicking sound with his tongue and his teeth like a squirrel will make when it's flicking its tail, excepting he's tapping his forefinger to his lip. *Snick, snick, snick.* "But . . . *snick* . . . that writing on the garage wall, well . . . that was no accident, *snick.*"

I just wait on him. He was gone on his train when that happened, and I guess I should've known when he got back he'd have something to say. But he's not to the asking-me-questions part, and I see no reason to encourage him.

He holds up a tie clip, examines it as if it were a diamond he'd never quite noticed before, one eye squinted down.

"Georgie tells me your cousin has a girl he's fond of. That right?" His voice is rough, and I realize he's not enjoying this like I thought he was.

"Yes."

"Well, that's nice." Voice still raspy. He puts the clip down and spreads his hands out like fans on the top of the dresser, feeling the wood.

"Dad, she quit him. There won't be any more trouble."

"That right?"

"Yes, sir."

"Billy understand that?" he asks, without turning to look at me.

"I think so. Yeah, he will."

"He understand there are folks more ignorant than most?"

"He understands."

Too quick he says, quick so I know he's unsettled, "But does he understand they can hurt him, and think they are doing the right thing while they're doing it?"

"Yeah," I say, slow. And then I say, "They really *do* think they are doing the right thing, don't they, Dad?"

His head swings round of its own, quick, and his eyes give off a bright flash I know is love before he can turn his head away again. "I just ride a train, son. I don't know."

I sit there a bit and I notice the very back of his head is starting to show a little hole of baldness. Maybe having so many kids is causing him to shed some like Rufus. I take in a big breath and blow it out and say, "Oh, heck, Dad, that's all right. I don't know either."

27.

We find Billy sitting on the curb in front of Mr. Woo's fish market. Sunday afternoon, late. They'll be closing soon. We're crossing the tracks, coming down Kern Street, when we spot him. "Okay, Georgie, don't say anything to shame him," I say.

"Why's he just sitting there?"

"'Cause he can't go to her house, and he's hoping she comes wandering by."

We come up on him and sit, one of us on each side of him,

Rufus at our feet. Nobody saying nothing. Seems we are all studying the neighborhood: The Imperial Theater, Nan's Golden Kitchen, Chow Fong's Men's Wear, Orange Grove Buddhist Temple with its big columns and thirty-eight concrete steps.

"Billy," I say, sighing just a little, but determined. I reach over and take his head in my hands and point him at myself and talk slow and sincere. "We know Mr. Koski is none of our concern. I just can't imagine him burning a tree—on account he's a biologist and on account he's . . . he's a person. A decent sort of somebody. And the Jensens have too much trouble to bother with discouraging us from seeing Veronica anymore. They got to know by now that scaring us off her ain't going to make her like Jeffers, either. Now they are living in their car, they don't have time to do much even if they are still mad about it. Aaaaaaaaand," I say, taking a big breath, "since Monsignor forbid us to tangle with them, we should let this thing go and just get on with Halloween."

He looks at me, one eye scrunched like I'm Judas. Shakes his head free of my hands.

"Billy, listen," I say, "in any case, you know that most in this whole town ain't comfortable with races mixing. And I don't know what it is we can do about that. You know if there was, I would help do it." I can feel my throat tighten up and I realize I mean it. Realize I'm sad and mad at the same time and those two feelings are like digesting a plate of honey and sand. I wonder if America will ever be like it is in social studies at school. It don't look like three kids and a slower-than-average dog sitting in the gutter on a street in Orange Grove, California, can make it so. "You can't see her no more," I add in a whisper.

"We ain't shaming you, Billy," Georgie says.

"Let me do this, will ya, Georgie?"

The Jensens should never have done the things they did, Billy signs.

"You are right. You are one hundred percent right."

Billy is scowling like I'm the one who did those things. I know he's just disappointed with the world.

All of a sudden, something comes looming up behind us throwing a huge shadow. We spin our heads round and there is this man with a ski mask on and black leotards and black boots, and sprouting off his arms are huge black and orange wings.

"I'm a butterfly!" Sammy Woo screeches through his ski mask, his eyes showing wide and happy.

People on the street are stopping and pointing and bumping into one another.

"Thought you was going as a dragon," I say, getting up.

"Found this in my aunt's attic. Better than a dragon."

"It's beautiful, Sammy," Georgie says. He's already up and

walking round him. I'm thinking Sammy is strange as usual, but today I see his brand of strange is beautiful.

Billy nods in appreciation too, but won't crack a smile.

"C'mon. C'mon, Billy, let's go see about our costumes," I say.

He gets up slow, and I take him by the elbow, which is a mistake 'cause he snaps his arm away, angry, but he goes with us. Sammy Woo skitters along behind us, arms pumping till we get to the tracks that split the two sides of town, where he hangs a U-turn and heads off, we waiting there a bit to watch him, Rufus barking at him as he flaps himself into the distance, alone, going his way home.

28.

I WAKE UP AFTER DREAMING ALL NIGHT OF wings of all kinds, flapping, and about a real bird I'd forgotten, this baby black starling that fell, wild and new, out of its nest and I'd found hopping in the leaves and nursed back to health, feeding it mash from an eyedropper until it was flying round the house and my mom said it had to go. I'd slunk around feeling sorry but knowing she was right and so took it outside riding on my finger. And it looked at me the way birds do. You know, with the head twisting one way and another so as to get a good look. I was as little as Georgie then.

It looked me straight in the eye and we held that way, just looking, like, *Who are you? What are you, really?* Neither of us old enough to know that answer, and truth is, I don't know it today. Then it jumped off my finger and slung up over the fence and was gone. I don't know why I have dreams or what they are supposed to do for a person, but to me they're an especially weird treat, a private one, and I don't usually tell them.

Anyway, I'm awake and living now, and sure enough, a whole week goes by and Veronica never once talks to Billy at school, no meeting him at lunch or afterward, either. I saw him once, saw him through the chain-link fence, like he was caged, sitting by himself at a metal table eating his lunch and watching the windows of one of the classrooms, and I knew Veronica was in there doing her homework instead of coming out, and I wondered if she couldn't help herself looking up to watch him back. I know she was. Know it the way I know things in dreams. Know it without seeing it whole. Know it 'cause it's a thing already whole, whether you can see it all the way yet or not.

Neither of the Jensens—not Jeffers at his school with Billy, nor Edgar at mine—take the time to bother us. In fact, we don't even see them and wonder if they are still going to school.

Billy isn't interested in any costume, either. Every day

after school I try hauling out our stuff for him to take stock of with me and see what else we might want or need, but he just wanders away. On Saturday I start getting itchy. It's the twenty-seventh of October on my mom's kitchen calendar, the one with a different saint for each month. It's Joseph again this month. Joseph gets a lot of play on church calendars on account he was the Lord's dad. I can see that, I guess, but I prefer the saints that did more spectacular stuff like flying round their chapels when they were praying hard and the Holy Spirit got into them.

Anyway, I see it is time that's flying now. I've had enough of Billy's moping. This morning I don't wake him. I find my gear and put it on. I got my soldier shirt and the long soldier jacket over that, the leather belt with the flap holster strapped to my waist and the cracked helmet on too. I stand over his bed and shout, "ATTEN-SHUN!"

Georgie shoots up from his sheets like a bottle rocket and comes down bouncing round in the corner by his little desk, his puny arms reaching this way and that to steady himself.

Billy snores.

Again I forget: He's deaf. I shake his shoulder a little. Little bit more. Shake it hard till his shoulders and head are rocking back and forth. Finally I take off my metal helmet and use it to give the front of his skull a good smart tap.

He sits up, slow as Frankenstein.

I put my helmet back on and sign, *Out of the rack, soldier.*

Billy rolls his eyes, yawns, and swings his legs off the bed and stands up.

I salute him, clicking my heels.

Then he socks me one, hard, in the teeth.

I go down and he's on top of me, his fists flinging down on me like rocks. I got my hands up trying to cover my face, and I can see Georgie in the corner, mouth hanging, eyes sparked. I can tell, in one of those flash moments where you see and understand things while you're only half paying attention, that he doesn't give a hoot who wins and is just enjoying having a front row seat.

I can't get a chance to hit back, 'cause Billy's surprised me and has me good, his knees jammed into my chest, smashing the air out of me, those rocks of his slamming the sides of my head now so quick all I can do is notice he's whacking me to some beat only he hears in his head, *whack-whack/whack-whack-whack/whack-whack/whack-whack-whack/whack-whack.* I feel sort of swimmy and thought-loose and like the sun going down, runny and dark. Then I feel his knees lifting off me, my ribs rising back into place and the air coming, quick, into the crunched paper sacks of my lungs.

Georgie is looking at me, face close. "Paolo," he says.

I can't say anything.

"You aren't going to die," he says. He's a doctor now and knows, isn't worried, just giving me the facts.

I blink, like, *Well, thanks, Doc.*

Billy's disappeared, up off of me and gone from the room.

I lie there and watch Georgie watch me from less than a half inch away, and I'm not mad at him or Billy. I know I just got the wind knocked out of me and nothing more, and all I am thinking about is the way that bird all those years ago jumped off my finger, how I felt and remembered all day the little push of his legs springing off me.

29.

SO BILLY WAS A STRANGER. Came and went when
he wanted and didn't speak to me or anyone. A pimple came
up, big, red, and angry, a little mountain that was snow-capped
white, right between his eyes, making him look mad and lovesick, which he was, I guess. I said hi a couple of times, but stopped
when he wouldn't even look at me. I knew he was sorry then,
and maybe ashamed. America had him and was squeezing. He
looked like something had bitten him, some small thing, maybe
near to invisible but huge with its poison. He had love in him

too, and didn't know how to get it out of him or if he wanted it out. You could tell he didn't know what to do. So he got mad and stayed that way.

My mom noticed. Looked him over good during meals but didn't ask. She wanted to, but held herself back. Italian ladies try not to get in the way of a boy who's trying to grow into a man. You are a man at thirteen if you are Italian, and though Billy is only ten and not Italian, he's being raised that direction.

My sisters would chitter and hop round and whisper to one another over their shoulders like squirrels when he passed. My dad and my brothers didn't see a thing except my two black eyes, which had blossomed out with a fine yellow edge to them that I was a little proud of. Hector snickered and made like he was a nutcase, jabbing his eyeballs out with his own fingers. My dad opened his mouth to speak once at dinner, thought better of it, and didn't. If he hadn't already talked to me, maybe things would've been different, and he knows it's Billy, not some others, that gave me those bruises. My dad's mostly a believer in not meddling, mostly figures kids grow up fine as long as there's food and a place to sleep and plenty of church. I can't say for sure if I disagree.

"What we going to do 'bout Halloween now, Paolo?" Georgie asks two days later, the evening of a Monday. We're sitting out front of our house, everything gloom and then the lights coming on, pretty and sparkly all over the neighborhood, a train in the distance letting go with its horn pulling, long, heart-tight, and lonesome.

"Well, we're going to go trick-or-treating and then to the carnival. Billy will come or he won't."

"He won't," Georgie says.

"I know."

"I know you know, Paolo," Georgie says to me, looking me straight in the eye, big brown eyes, feeling Italian and sorry.

"Tell you what, Georgie. Suppose we go over Miss Farisi's right now and get that tank of yours?"

At that his face goes the color of the sky, which is cloud-smoked but bright. If he knew what it was, he'd be chortling Italian opera. We get up and go. "You know, it's only tomorrow and then the next day is Halloween," he says. He's little-kid excited, the way he should be.

"Yeah, and I got my costume all squared away. Wait till you see," I say, maybe just a little bit excited myself.

We hustle though the neighborhoods, going the thirteen or so blocks till we hit country, crossing out through the fields. I got my four-battery police flashlight, and it sends out a long oval of light in front of us, though with the moon we hardly need it. We skirt round the parking lot of the Sun-Maid raisin plant in case the Jensens are there in their car and come up on Miss Farisi's house in no time.

Georgie goes to the front window and taps. I can't blame him for that. We are not used to showing up at people's front doors. We are so used to looking in windows and poking round garages that he's forgotten we could just go to the front door proper this time. Miss Farisi must have heard him, 'cause she swings the door open and says, "Hello?"

I step into the light on her porch, and Georgie comes crashing through the shrubs to join me. Has bits of bush stuck in his hair.

She just looks at us.

I splash the flashlight beam over Georgie and then put it on myself. "It's us, Miss Farisi."

"Yes, I see that." She's frowning some concern to herself but not saying it. "Well . . . come in."

We step into her living room. Mr. Edmund is sitting there in an easy chair with only the back of his head showing. He's got a book open on his lap. He doesn't turn or say hello, and so I pretend he is invisible, since I'm not stupid and that seems to be the wanted thing.

Miss Farisi says, "Come now, into the kitchen."

We go, following her like geese. Georgie is craning his neck round and saying, "Hey, Mr. Edmund. Hello? Mr. Edmund?

Mr. Edmund!" The swinging door to the kitchen almost swats Georgie's rear as it closes behind him. I have the feeling Miss Farisi helped that door close a bit faster than it would have on its own.

"Hush," I say to him.

"It's all right, Paolo." Miss Farisi sighs.

"Miss Farisi, we want—," Georgie begins.

"Your costume. Of course. I just thought you'd be coming tomorrow for it. Stay here. I'll get it." And she swishes out the door we just came in.

"She's mad," Georgie says.

"Not mad. She's just feeling private tonight."

"What for, private?"

"Well, for a teacher, she is having a lot of company for one night."

"One person?"

"Just forget about it, and be sure to say thanks for your costume," I say.

"You don't have to tell me that."

Miss Farisi comes in backward, loaded down with a green tank with a cannon sticking out its front and a white star stenciled on its side. She pivots sideways and puts it on the kitchen table.

"Wow," I say.

Georgie looks like he is about to cry at its beauty. He slides his chubby hand along one side of it. "It . . . it's . . ." He is looking at Miss Farisi.

She seems to relax and and pats him on the head. "I thought it turned out pretty well myself. Here, hop up on the table and let's see how it fits."

Georgie scrambles up on a kitchen chair. Miss Farisi holds open the slit in the back of the tank, and he sticks his head and shoulders and arms in. He wrestles around in there a bit, squirming himself situated, and then stands up. And there he is, a U. S. of A. tank with Georgie legs sticking out the bottom, right there on Miss Farisi's kitchen table.

"Put your head forward and you will be able to see out the front machine-gun holes!" Miss Farisi says, loud.

"I can. I CAN!" he shouts.

"Okay, okay, we can hear you," I say.

Georgie turns himself around and steps down off of the table onto the chair, then down to the floor.

"Oh, that's good," says Miss Farisi, her hands coming together in a silent clap. "You should be able to get around pretty well. But promise me, Paolo, you will go with him wherever he goes to be sure of his safety."

"I already do that all the time anyway, Miss Farisi."

"Oh. Well . . . good."

Georgie wants to wear his tank home, but we talk him out of it, since it wouldn't do to spoil his surprising folks come Wednesday. I help him get his tank off, and then we sit around Miss Farisi's kitchen till she thinks to offer us some cookies and milk, which we are polite enough to accept.

While we are munching, I tell her some about Billy. About Veronica. About kids at school and about her dad not letting her see him. She seems to know some of it already. Maybe Veronica told her or maybe just 'cause she is a teacher of the kind that pays attention to what the kids at school are up to.

"Miss Farisi, I just don't get why Billy is so mad. You'd think lovesick would make him more sorrowful than mad."

"Maybe he has good reason to be angry," she says, soft.

"Yeah?"

"Maybe it is not just that he can't see Veronica, but why he can't see her."

"'Cause she's too young?"

"Paolo, we both know it's more than that. Don't we?" She blinks her big, pretty, intelligent eyes. And they're wet just a little with some kind of soft fury, the way ladies get sometimes.

30.

I'M FEELING LOUSY THAT I EVER ONCE
thought of Veronica as Red Chinese or Chinese at all. I know I
told Billy I was sorry for that a long time ago, but I see I didn't
really understand it. Something about Miss Farisi hating it
makes me hate it too. Hate thinking about a person's skin. Hate
thinking different is the same as wrong. I see that even a person
as nice and smart and helpful as myself could have some of that
judging in them and not even know it.

I even think about how everybody and myself, too, thinks

down on the Jensens, calls them hillbillies and never gives a thought that that might not be what they want to hear. I think of my grandpa and know I want to have an America like his America. I feel sick in my stomach to think he might think of me as a judger of men, so I decide I want to stop thinking of it for a while or maybe just forget. Halloween makes me forget.

Wednesday is a school day, but Georgie and I make it a holiday, heading off for school with Rufus and then doubling back and going to our spot in the orchard where our burnt-down tree sticks up, black and pointed like a giant bottle rocket that blew up and sizzled before it got off the ground. Luke and Sammy are supposed to meet us here at four o'clock. Then we are going trick-or-treating for a couple of hours and then over to the carnival, where Georgie will have to help me on cleanup crew since who knows what's what with Billy. I went ahead and put together a costume for him of what was left of Mrs. Sweeney's WWI stuff; along with the pillowcases I have for our treats, I have it in a big paper shopping sack just in case.

Yes, I will look out for your treats if you have trouble seeing out of your tank, yes, you can trick-or-treat at our house and at Grandpa and Grandma Leonardo's, yeah, we will wait for Sammy. . . . No, I don't think the Jensens will recognize you in your costume, no, I won't let Luke trip you, and he wouldn't want to trip you anyway. Georgie is starting to get on my nerves, and I see one of the reasons Billy is such good company, what with his not being able to talk. I miss him.

We've been sitting there most of the day just watching, Uncle Charlie-style, the clouds and swarms of gnats boxing in circles. Georgie sits with his arm around his tank, Rufus sleeping next to the tank, once in a while his eyes rolling round in his head looking us all over, knowing something is up and looking as if he's thinking, *I'm keeping it secret that I'll be ready whenever it is stuff starts happening.*

"Paolo, do you think I will grow up and find someone like Miss Farisi to marry me?"

"I thought you were going to marry *her.*"

"I think she already has somebody taller picked out."

He has his lower lip stuck out and his eyes squinted, measuring out the hard facts of life.

"I can't say for sure, Georgie. Women might not like a fellow who asks a million questions all the time."

"Why not?"

"Well, they might find it irritating."

"Why's that?"

"Well, maybe 'cause it might make you sound stupider than you are."

"Who would think I am more stupid than I already am?"

"Beats me."

"You know I know lots of stuff, don't you, Paolo?"

"Yeah. I'm the one who taught you every bit of knowledge you have."

"I know things even you don't know."

"No kidding. Well, you make a list of those things and you give it to me sometime. It'll be fascinating to read."

"I could just tell them to you."

"You could, but . . ."

"I know some things especially that I haven't told you yet."

"Really? You sure you know one whole thing."

"Yep. A big thing. I can tell you, but I don't want you to let it spoil Halloween."

I snap my head over bird-sharp and eye him. When Georgie starts in like this, he usually has some kind of shocker. I know this from times past. I take a little breath. I say, soft, "I won't let it spoil Halloween." I say it like a promise, quiet.

He scrounges round in his pocket. "You remember the night Billy got smacked with that rock?"

"Yeah . . ."

"Mom got the roll of film from Dad's Brownie camera back from Woolworth's yesterday." He jabs a scrunched-up, wrinkled-bad little photograph at me.

I grab it and smooth it, best I can, on the flat of my hand.

"Remember I had that camera that night? I took a picture when we were on the grass by the streetlight."

The picture is crinkled. What must be Billy and Rufus and me is out-of-focus-smeary because we are too close to the camera, but what *is* there, just inside the light spread out from the lamppost, in the background, are the bleached-bright faces of Matthew and Mark Cheng.

31.

SOMETIMES YOU KNOW A THING AND YOU got to pretend that you don't. You got to pretend 'cause you don't know yet what to do with your knowing. And you don't know yet how telling what you know might change the world or if you are ready for that change. And sometimes telling could hurt people you have no intention of hurting. Sometimes it is like all of those things at once, and maybe that is why I say nothing, except, "I'm going to keep this picture, Georgie, and you are not going to say anything about anything."

The way I say it, as if the sky might crumble down right this instant into a million dark pieces like the end of the world, the way it does every evening though nobody seems to really notice, is why Georgie just nods his head and means it, I can tell. But he says, weak, "I told you I know things you don't. And I—"

"Just hush with your knowing! All right?"

Georgie looks about to cry, bottom lip a fat slug arching its back, his eyes little dark pots of paint.

"Ah, Georgie, you did good," I say.

He swallows hard and smiles, one tear working its way down his cheek.

"Here, let me help you get your tank on. It's already about four o'clock." He likes that, and we get it on him. I slip inside my itchy wool jacket and strap my leather belt and holster to myself. I put my helmet on, and I notice I am a little bit trembly. I have the gas mask in my bag with the stuff for Billy. "Let's go, Georgie," I say.

"Okay," he says, all hollow and from a long way off.

We start leaving and then Georgie's tank swings its cannon round on me. "What about Sammy and Luke?" he says. I can see one of his eyes through a machine-gun hole.

"We'll run into them on the way. Besides, we said four o'clock and it's that now."

Then I see a dark flapping way out in the distance of that grove, a black flapping that looks like a giant insect that is wounded and unable to fly, its wings pumping, trying to get free of this world that is too heavy for it, get free and swim up into the air it was made for, and of course it is Sammy. Some kind of bush is following him, and I know it has to be a cotton plant and so Luke is with him.

We hook up and everybody admires each other's costume, but there is no kidding ourselves it is Sammy's that is the best. Georgie's is very cool, and mine is okay. Luke just looks like he took some cotton branches and duct-taped them to himself, which is what he did. He looks more like he's escaped from Stockton State Mental Hospital than a trick-or-treater. I keep looking his eyes over to see if he knows about his brothers and can't tell. My brothers do all kinds of things that I never know nothing about.

The world's got just a hint of dark to it, so we get started. I pull my gas mask on and all goes yellow. We go to Grandpa Leonardo's first. He swings open the door and shouts, "It's-a trick-a fo you. It's-a treat!"

"Uh, that's our part to say, Grandpa," I tell him, quiet-like.

He leans forward to listen closely, then shakes his head, "Oh, yes-a, yes." Then he waits for us to say it. But we've been thrown off our rhythm.

"Grandpa, could you shut the door so's we can try again?"

He nods his head, *Yes, yes.* Shuts the door. Then it explodes open and he says, "Surprise! I'm-a surprised!"

Everybody is quiet.

Grandpa is looking round at us, confused.

Sammy Woo says, "Trick or treat, Grandpa Georgie!"

Grandpa lights up at that and starts hauling bags of candy out onto the porch. Grandpa owns a grocery store, and his house and his garage are chock-full of goodies. He has three of his very own freezers in the garage laid up with chocolate ice cream. I suppose if the Russians went mad and sent us the bomb, we could live on chocolate ice cream for most of a year. All that stuff is for us.

Grandpa fills all of our bags right to the top with gumdrops and Tootsie Rolls and lemon drops and butterscotch candy. We trudge out of there like a caravan of desert bandits. I'm lugging my haul and Georgie's, too. We start to see half shadows of other kids flitting round the block and know then Halloween is on, full tilt.

We go to our house next. Hector answers the door. "No, we already take the paper," he announces. Shuts the door.

I give the door bell eighty or ninety more rings.

My mom answers, Italian-mad at all the ringing. "It's us!" I say, quick, so's she'll calm down.

"Can you guess if I'm Georgie?" Georgie says from way down in his tank.

"Trick or treat!" says Sammy Woo.

My mom looks tired, her hair is sticking out this way and that, and I know she's been ironing and rushing as usual. Maybe she has duties to do with the Ladies Altar Society, as it is Wednesday. They might even have a booth at the carnival. I don't think so. She never said. She probably wants a night in, anyway. She rummages in her apron pockets and comes out with little tiny boxes of raisins that she drops in our bags. My mom thinks raisins are candy, since Grandpa didn't always own that store and back in her day a box of raisins was a treat.

"You look out for Georgie," is all she says, heartfelt, before closing the door.

We go up and down our block and the next one and the next. It's full dark now, and I have one hand on Georgie's cannon to lead him. I tied my two pillow sacks of candy together and have them round my neck like saddlebags. We figure out that old people give the best and the most candy but take the longest to get to the door. Most of them have a wiener dog or a rat terrier and Halloween is their favorite holiday too. They go quivery-mad at the commotion, jumping on couches and sticking their heads out of the drapes and hopping backward and spinning round in circles. I like a big dog myself but wouldn't mind owning a little firecracker one too, if I didn't think Rufus would get tired of the yapping and eat it.

"Paolo, I'm tired," Georgie says.

"We hardly got started," I say.

"Paolo, I'm tired," he says.

"We waited all year for this and you want to quit?"

"Paolo, I'm tired."

Once a little kid gets going on a sentence like that he won't let it go, even if you put torture to him directly. It's like a little-kid brain has just enough cogs and wheels to go one way only, and it's too hard for their little machine to reverse its direction so that's that.

"Okay, okay," I say. We do have a ton of candy anyway. Luke and Sammy are good with knocking off and heading to the carnival. On the way, we stop at our house and take our goodies out to the garage and hide them under a tarp. We got to hide them, since a certain Ernie and Hector have been known to get into my Halloween stuff on account they are too old to trick-or-treat themselves. Luke and Sammy leave theirs, too.

When we are rumpling the tarp just right so it looks like nothing unusual, I say to Luke, "You don't suppose your brothers will be at the carnival, do you?"

His eyes jerk back and forth, quick like he's thinking,

thinking a little too quick, and he seems to shrug to play it off. But I catch it. Gives me a feeling in my stomach like a stone sinking down, sinking fast through a deep, murky lake, straight down and hitting bottom, making a secret explosion in the mud.

32.

A FIRECRACKER POPS, AND PINWHEELS OF sparklers spin, mad-wild, making a quick fading universe of stars on the back of my eyeballs. Kids are running round in their costumes, going back and forth from booth to booth, half of them squirrel-cheeked with cake and candy, the other half screeching and laughing. Monsignor is sitting above a tank of water, and the men from the parish are paying one whole dollar a throw with a hardball to try and hit a bull's-eye that will send him splashing down. Monsignor has on black swimming trunks and a black T-shirt and looks strange up there. He's already rat-drowned and spongy from going in again and again, 'cause those men have been throwing baseballs since they were kids and know how. They aren't doing it for meanness but 'cause Monsignor will be after them if they don't spend their dollars after he's gone to all the bother to get baptized over and over and him not even wearing his collar.

You wouldn't recognize the church parking lot with all that is strung round. Piñatas hanging from wires, little left-over Christmas bulbs, ribbons and flags of all kinds, but most especially pretty are the paper lanterns—blue, red, and black—lit and making the whole place mellow and heart-washed with pretty. Mr. Woo is there inspecting them, walking round them, neck-bent and approving. He's got what must be Mrs. Woo and some more Woos with him, all moving along like ducks. I wish my mom or my brothers were here so's someone would talk to them.

I notice Mrs. Ogilbee and her buck-toothed daughter, Cheryl Ann, who are running the fruit drink stand, give them all a frown when they all duck-up in a line for punch. Then I see Grandpa Leonardo. I should have known he'd leave Grandma to do the trick-or-treaters and come be with his buddies. He walks up and shakes Mr. Woo's hand and pats him once on the back, lightly. Mr. Woo is bowing and smiling. Then some more Sons of Italy, pals of Grandpa, not one of them more than four feet tall, come over and do likewise. Everybody looks pretty uncomfortable, stiff like they'd shatter if you touched them, but they are, all of them, trying. I wish hard that Billy could be here and see too. See Grandpa and the carnival. I keep an eye peeled for him in case he is about somewhere.

We see Miss Farisi done up as a lion tamer with blousy trousers and jackboots. Mr. Edmund is supposed to be a lion she has on a chain. He's got whiskers penciled on his cheeks, which are powdered white, and dots on his nose, which is colored black, and he's wearing all yellow and a dog collar. He'd look more the part if he was on all fours instead of just standing next to her, grinning. A couple of Altar Society ladies are whispering hard, eyes swinging from the Woos to Mr. Edmund and Miss Farisi. Folks in our town think they own everyone and everything in it, and the truth is, with their sharp little tongue-lashing, they do keep it all herded pretty tight.

There's lots there that don't go to our church, 'cause it's a good carnival and all are welcome. There are booths selling tamales and deep-fried chimichangas and booths with Tennessee apple cobbler; the DiCiccio brothers are twirling pizzas; there's even egg rolls with rice, and Mr. Murphey is selling Coca-Cola out of the bed of his pickup, which is filled with mounds of chipped ice. I know bottles of Guinness beer are snugged down deep in there too. The men and Monsignor will polish them off later. Ernie says Monsignor figures that being a dad is hard on a man, and he never begrudges a fellow a bit of relaxing as long as he gives most of his check to his wife. I wish my dad could be there too, with the others, but he's on his train somewhere between here and Kansas earning that check. Anyway, tonight you can eat and drink yourself round the whole world without ever getting off of the corner of Mariposa and R Street.

Luke and Sammy decide they would rather not learn all about careers in modern sanitation, no matter how important it could be to their futures, and they leave Georgie and me standing next to a trash can with its own little trailer. Kind of a wheelchair for a garbage can. We know to go to the shed behind the church to get our garbage-picking sticks. They are these broom-handle things with little nails sticking out of one end. We are to go round spear-fishing paper wrappers and such.

I got to get Georgie out of his tank, which we leave in the shed. It 'bout breaks his heart, but he won't go against what Monsignor has told us. Well, what I told him Monsignor has told us: It's God's will we stab all those papers and keep the place clean.

"Paolo, I thought it was Billy was who supposed to be your helper," Georgie says.

"Yeah, but he's not here and you're next in line."

"I'm not in any line," he says.

"Georgie, it's just the same as if you were the little brother of the king of England and your older brother got sick or died or decided to marry a divorced woman with beady eyes and thin lips. Well, you'd be next in line to be king."

"Billy isn't my brother, he's my cousin."

"Same thing."

"I don't think being a garbage man is the same thing, Paolo."

"Why, of course it is. Besides, you ain't a garbage man, you are a handpicked servant of the Lord."

"Paolo, how come the Lord needs so many servants?"

"It's a big world."

"I'd as soon be his friend," he says, eyes scrunched serious.

"You got me for a friend, Georgie."

"I know," he mumbles to himself. "I know."

We set about doing God's will and actually start having fun with the stabbing. Pretty soon we forget ourselves and are sword fighting when I back right into a guy in a white sheet with two black holes cut for eyes. Supposed to be a ghost, I imagine. He's got a fellow with him with a gunny sack over his head tied with a string and a cap pistol stuck in his belt. I suppose he's a bank robber or something. Then I get this feeling like somebody sewed my lungs together and is pulling the threads tight, 'cause I realize it's the Jensens—they're the right size and have cheap costumes like those two would. I forget myself and drop my stick.

I can't say excuse me for bumping them or even say anything at all. I just stand there waiting on them. Georgie senses trouble and comes up alongside of me. He picks up my spear and holds his and mine up high by the ends like he's one of those bullfighters down in Mexico, ready to stick one of them in the back or the neck. Georgie can be dangerous, 'cause he's too little to know he could really hurt someone bad without meaning to. Rufus walks round back of them snuffling their rumps.

"Have you seen Billy?" says one.

"Or Veronica?" says the other.

"Veronica has been missing since early this morning," says the first one.

I realize I haven't seen Billy since yesterday. I realize, too, it's Mark and Matt Cheng's voices that are asking the questions.

33.

WE COULD JUST FLY AWAY, BILLY.

My hand's shaky, reading it. Reading the note Georgie found in his bed this morning, decoded, and is now showing to me and the Chengs on account we are all talking about them. It's written in the same girl handwriting as before.

"You can't be mad, Paolo, even though you said before, enough of my knowledge." He doesn't know what, but he knows by everyone's quiet and my trembly hands that something's wrong.

"Not mad, Georgie," I whisper.

Luke and Sammy Woo have seen us bunched up and come over. Sammy Woo says, "They not around here. I looked."

Matthew and Mark have taken off their costumes, and their faces look milk-splashed with fright. They look, in some way, young as Georgie.

"We need to tell a person about this," I hear myself saying. "An adult person. Miss Farisi, maybe." I don't sound like myself at all.

"Tell them what, exactly?" Mark says, looking down on me.

"Tell them about persons that would burn a tree house down and paint nasty notes on somebody's garage on account he doesn't think his sister should be making friends with a kid from Appalachia," I whisper in a fast, angry hiss so's Georgie doesn't hear me.

Matthew takes my elbow and says, "Come over here a second, will you, Paolo?" He's looking at Georgie and Sammy and Luke and then back at me. His eyes are saying, *Please just do this little thing, come over where we can talk, private.*

So Mark and Matt and I walk over near one corner of the cathedral that with its two long spires towers over the parking lot where all is going on. It's dark there and cooler, too, only the outlines of those two peaks are visible. "Paolo, try to understand what I am going to tell you. Okay? Will you try?" It's Mark's voice, and it's just a sound in a cold, dark barrel.

"All right."

"People here don't treat Chinese the way they do others. You aren't Chinese and you don't know. No matter how much we are Americans, there are plenty that don't see it that way."

His hand on my elbow softens its grip. His voice could be anybody's.

"Everybody in America comes from someplace and they mostly join in and get along," I say.

"Do they? Paolo, if you are from Italy or from Sweden or someplace like that, you can blend in when you want. But if you are Chinese, you always look Chinese. And if you *look* a particular way they think is bad—to a whole lot of people then that's what you *are*: bad. Period."

I never thought about what he is saying. How you could not tell I am Italian or Appalachian just by looking. I feel kind of sick in my stomach. I think of throwing up, and then for no reason I think of that whale in the Bible spitting up, spitting up Jonah, and I imagine us down in the belly of that thing, all dark and only our voices swimming round.

"We just didn't want our sister to get hurt."

"Billy would never hurt anyone," I say.

"Yeah, but someone else might. Someone who wouldn't think it was such a good idea for a Chinese girl and a kid like Billy to be walking around town holding hands."

Before I pass out, which is what I am feeling like doing, I say, "Turns out you were the ones doing the hurting. You know, *you* cracked Billy's tooth. *You* started a *fire*."

"We threw that rock. It was stupid." Mark is talking fast, but he's serious, and like it or not he's making a kind of sense to me.

"We didn't think it was going to hurt anybody." It's Matthew talking this time. I notice that and also that I have not passed out.

"We weren't going to burn anything, Paolo. We went over to your tree house to maybe mess up some of your stuff. We lit matches to see in the dark, and it just happened."

"Just happened," I say.

"I swear, Paolo."

I can picture Billy and me doing something just as stupid without meaning to. I see us breaking into Mrs. Sweeney's garage, Mr. Koski's truck. But I say, "And you accidentally painted on our garage and left that match there?" There's the taste of a bitter penny in my mouth.

"No." Matthew's voice comes, sudden, from behind me.

He must have moved. I can see the carnival lights all awhirl only a couple of hundred feet away, like a party boat anchored just off the shore of a huge night lake, the voices coming over the water like wind chimes tinkling and seagulls crying.

"No, Paolo, we did that on purpose. We were scared after the fire. Scared that we'd get caught and shame our family."

"Scared we'd go to jail," Mark says.

Suddenly I'm shuffling memories like photographs in my head: My folks, my sisters. My grandpa. I understand.

"We thought we could make it seem like it was somebody else."

"You thought you could make it seem like the Jensens," I say.

"We thought we could make it seem like the Jensens," Mark says, slow, shamed, like I am Monsignor hearing their confession, and I realize I don't have what it takes, will never grow up to be a priest.

34.

WHAT I WANTED TO KNOW WAS WHETHER Luke knew what his brothers had been doing. I guess I had started to like him and he'd been accepted as part of our crew, and I wanted to think he'd been a genuine friend. Mark told me for sure Luke hadn't a clue, and I was glad of it. It was Luke who figured things out then, though. Figured out quicker than I thought a kid could what we needed to do and how what we needed to do could be done without grown folks. Well, without them knowing all that we did.

Said it was simple. Said he believed some part of his mind had been working on it ever since that afternoon at Miss Farisi's when Veronica told the story of the lanterns. Taking care not to scare Georgie, he said something like, "The only spot round here that somebody could jump from, could . . . fly from . . . could fly, say, a kite from, is Reedley Leap." Reedley Leap is a bluff that juts out of the very first foothill of the Sierra.

Matt chimed in, telling how that was right and how it was just out back from their grandma's place in Reedley. I said how Billy and Veronica could've walked the almost ten miles to Reedley, if they'd set out this morning. Georgie said if we were going there he'd rather not walk, and Mr. Koski's panel truck could carry us all.

We find Mr. Koski talking to Mr. Fields and the both of them talking to Mrs. Sweeney, who is running a booth selling used books, which is as dumb as it sounds. No kid in his right mind would buy a book on Halloween night. But when it comes to old folks, I know you can't teach them a thing. They get stubborn and decide that for the rest of their days the world is just going to have to be the way they'd always wanted it, and they start acting however they please and saying whatever occurs to them and giving you a glare if you even let on in the slightest that maybe they've gone mad as a hatter. Anyway, she's laughing and having a heck of a grand time talking and selling books that nobody's buying.

Mr. Koski is buying those laughs and smiles of hers, though. Mr. Fields is smoking a cigar about a foot long and wearing a genuine Stetson hat and listening, all smiles too. He's got a handlebar mustache and walks like he's balancing an invisible barrel between his legs because besides being the shop teacher, he raises horses. I'm itching to interrupt them and get going, but they see us and seem to be making a point of finishing their talking first. I start thinking about Mr. Fields to keep myself from exploding, which wouldn't be the best thing to do around Mr. Fields. He has a reputation that advises you not get him riled. Ernie says Mr. Fields is better with creatures than people, maybe even a genius with dumb animals. Said he had a horse that blew up on him once, out of nowhere, threw him clear across his corral. Mr. Fields just walked back, slow, to that horse, slapping dust from his britches, and leaned close and whispered into that horse's ear. That horse's ear flickered like a wind-spooked leaf, and it went back to his stall all of its own and stayed there for three days and wouldn't eat, and when it came out it never threw anybody again, ever. Ernie says you could tell which horse it is, 'cause it's cross-eyed permanent now, from taking care to never look Mr. Fields in the eye.

Finally Mrs. Sweeney finishes what she's been telling, and

they all turn like one person to us, where they know darn well we've been squirming. We explain that we have to go get Veronica from Reedley, where she is visiting her grandma. We tell how Veronica is needed at home to help with little John Cheng, who's caught a fever, and on account Veronica's dad is working tonight, he can't fetch her. We ask Mr. Koski to give us all a ride. Mr. Koski's eyes light up scientific-like at the word "fever," and he says, "Okay, okay. Well, c'mon, then." He tips his hat at Mrs. Sweeney, nods to Mr. Fields, and we go.

So it's Georgie and I and Mr. Koski in the front seat and Matt and Mark and Luke and Sammy crunched into the back of his panel truck. Everybody has taken his costume off except Sammy. He's got his wrapped round Rufus, gentle. He thinks he is hiding Rufus from Mr. Koski, but he ain't.

Since Mr. Koski is a biologist, I believe he could smell a dog a mile away and probably know its age and who its daddy was and what it had for breakfast and whether it was sick or not—just from that smell. I'm not a biologist, but I can tell Rufus hasn't had a bath in a couple of months. But Mr. Koski isn't bothering about Rufus being along for the ride. You can trust a man that'll suffer the bother and mess of a dog. Don't know why that is, but it's true. Ernie never told me that. I told myself.

Mr. Koski is a careful driver, or else I'm too worried about what's with Veronica and Billy, 'cause it seems he's driving painful-slow. I want Mr. Koski to let those big eight cylinders go and suck air and gasoline the whole time instead of just nosing along at the speed limit like he does. He doesn't know how serious things might be, and I'm still too scared to tell him. My heart's rabbit-thumping, and I think it'll never happen, but we do get there, to Reedley. It is about one-fourth the size of Orange Grove City, maybe less. It has one main street and five or six blocks spoking off of that, a railroad station and the Kings River splitting the whole town right down the middle. Fact is, the only reason Reedley got to be a town is that it used to be where stuff got loaded off barges from the river.

We crawl through main street: a Bank of America, post office, barbershop, the usual stuff, the only traffic a Ford pickup we follow for a bit, faces of some kids smiling and giggling and poking above the sides of the bed like pumpkins.

Finally Mr. Koski pulls up the dirt drive that leads to Grandma Cheng's house. She's just outside town on a couple of acres that's growing dirt and doing a fine job of it. She's got a little place and frilly curtains in the windows that are seeping a buttery light. Mr. Koski shuts his Dodge down and says he'll wait in the car, flicks on the dome light, pulls out a book called *Radiosonde Data Collection*, and starts reading. I almost ask what it's about and then realize he will tell me if I ask and so don't.

We run up to the front door and go in, except Rufus. Luke and Mark have the job of chit-chatting with Mrs. Cheng and keeping her from suspicions and Mr. Koski, too, should he end up wanting to come in. Georgie and Matt and Sammy and I trot right out the back door and run up an old beaten path that snakes up from her place, glad to be out of the truck and moving now as fast as we can. Grandma Cheng doesn't even notice we came through her house. Luke and Mark are talking her ears off, talking loud, her TV loud too, on account of she's hard of hearing, I guess.

There's moon and my flashlight, and we know exactly where we want to look and don't want to waste one second getting there. Rufus comes bouncing up behind us, happy that he's right—there is some kind of game going on.

That dirt path ribbons up over the rise there and then flattens out. We are on the little tabletop they call Reedley Leap. It's rolling foothill on the side we came up and then a flat blacksmith's anvil at the top and then a couple-hundred-foot drop down the other. Our little path weakens and fails near the edge. No Billy or Veronica. Just some big hammerhead clouds swimming up in the darkness, backlit by moonlight and stars.

"There ain't any birds flying round here," Georgie says.

"Birds usually sleep at night, Georgie," Matt tells him.

"There aren't any lanterns," Georgie says.

I realize I don't know what he understands and what he doesn't, and I am beginning to ask the same thing about myself.

Sammy sits down near the edge of the cliff and Georgie joins him. I look at Matt and we both blow air out our lungs, shrug, and sit too, though it feels awful to me to do it, since my mind is telling my body it should be running; I can feel my hands, all ten fingers, trembling. We are looking back at the valley, all the little lights sipping darkness. "In the morning, maybe we'll see buzzards circling," Georgie says.

That makes me feel like somebody slapped me. Matt looks like he might get sick all over himself. "There won't be no buzzards, Georgie," I say.

"There can't be," Matt says, his voice gravelly, low.

"Matt, did you know we are in North America?" Georgie says.

"Uh. Yeah, I do."

I'm just listening to this one, since I am stumped as to what to do.

"Well, we are. I know for sure," Georgie says.

"That's great, Georgie," Matt says, maybe glad to be talking about something other than vultures.

"Hector showed me. In the toilet."

"What?" I say.

"If you flush the toilet and you live above the equator, the water swirls counterclockwise. Same with birds, Paolo. They circle round counterclockwise too."

Matt and I don't say a thing.

"If you were down under the equator, things swirl the other way. Hector showed me in the bathroom the other day. If we stay here till morning we could see if the birds circle the way they are supposed to."

"And if they don't?" I say.

"They will," Georgie says.

"You going to ship them down to South America if they don't? Georgie, do you know—"

"Matthew? Matt?" It's Veronica's voice, and it's coming out of the dark just below us!

"Veronica!" Matt shouts.

"Matthew, be careful. Don't come to the edge!"

But Sammy, Georgie, Matt, and I have already jumped up and done just that and are standing, wobbly, peeking over, pebbles of dirt coming off the toes of our shoes. I point my flashlight. There, a ways down, are the upturned faces of Billy and Veronica, eyes scared, lips shivering.

35.

Bits of dirt clods rain down on them, and they keep dropping their heads to keep the stuff out of their eyes. Billy is holding Veronica close to him and leaning back against the cliff face to weight them there. He can't sign me a thing. But I see fast enough the fix they're in. I swing my little sword of light back and forth to size things up.

They are standing just ten or so feet below us, standing on a bit of ledge maybe eight to ten inches wide, and that cliff face is almost as dry as a brittle old cake and wanting to crumble. "Get back!" I shout to everyone. "Back!" They do, except Matthew, who can't take his eyes off his sister. I snap off the light so he can't see and say, soft and steady, "Matt, we got to step back so's we don't send what we're standing on down onto them."

"Right," he says. "Right." I hear him move back.

"Matt!" Veronica shouts, the light going out scaring her, I think.

"I'm here, Veronica!"

"We are going to get you out of there!" I yell. Then to Matt I say, "We need rope. We need Mr. Koski. We're going to need all of us to get enough weight on our end."

Matt says, "Paolo, even together, even with Sammy and Koski, we're going to have a heck of a time lifting them off there."

We hear Veronica sobbing, soft. We realize that our shouting hadn't been necessary. They are so close they can hear us talking.

"Truck. Mr. Koski's truck will pull them," Sammy says, suddenly there at my shoulder.

"Sammy!" I'm glad he's there. "Sammy, get Mr. Koski," I say. I can't see him, but I know he's heard me and can sense he's already gone.

"Matt, this ledge is coming apart." Veronica's voice sounds very frightened but very sane. "This afternoon we came down and it was wide enough for us to sit on. We just wanted to sit . . . together . . . by ourselves . . . and watch the lights. I'm . . . sorry, Matt." She breaks into more sobbing, the air chuffing hard in and out of her throat.

"It's going to be all right," Matt says, his voice choking. I know there is nothing worse than feeling something is your fault and all the while the one you hurt telling you *they're* sorry.

"I got rope, Paolo," Georgie says. "I got it from the back porch." He's got a coil as big as he is. He drops it, it thumping in the dirt.

"That's good. You did good, Georgie. Now you stay back, okay?"

"Okay, Paolo. I'll stay back."

Suddenly headlights are stabbing the darkness, crazy around us, bouncing from the ground into the night sky. It's Mr. Koski and that Dodge panel truck of his jumping toward us, finally moving full throttle, coming cross-country, climbing the rise. He comes to a halt maybe thirty yards from us, the truck slumping into the dirt. But we have light now, all over us. Mr. Koski runs heavy, through the powdery soil, his felt hat flying off his head, his beard ragged, eyes bright and piercing as an owl's. "It's stalled-out there. But I'll get some wood under the wheels, and it should be good to pull the few feet we need. Right? They're only down a few feet, right?"

"Yeah," I say, snapping out of my daze. I realize Mr. Koski is trusting us to know what to do. I also see he is just now rethinking that.

"Let me see," says Mr. Koski, then throws himself on the ground and edges toward the lip of the cliff and peers over. I drop down and crawl up next to him and again send a tunnel of light through the darkness to their faces. Veronica is weeping, and Billy's head and shoulders are pressed back as far as he can snug himself and Veronica into the mountain. Sand trickles off from around their shoes, sifting down the cliffside.

"Get this end of the rope around them. Can you do that?"

"Yeah," comes Matt's voice from over my shoulder.

"Fine. That's fine." That's all Mr. Koski says, as if to himself, and he is gone back toward the truck with the other end of the line, his figure jerky, coat flapping, black in the light of the headlamps.

"Give me the rope," Matt says. He takes our end and, quick, fashions a lasso. "Drop the light on them," he says with a voice dead serious, past afraid and all the way to cold terror, I think.

Then Mark is there, huffing from running up the slope. "Here!" he shouts. "I'll do this!"

"Move back from the edge, Mark," Matt says. "Paolo and I have this." He says that with authority of some kind, and Mark just obeys and steps back. I keep the light on those two and Matt drops his lasso. It lands like a snake over Veronica's shoulders.

"Lift your arms," I say, not wanting to spook her. "Let the rope come down under your armpits." She wants to, you can tell she wants to, but Billy would have to let go of her and she or he or both of them could slip free and be lost. I look at Billy. He understands. He pulls her like a dancer, switching places, her arms going up and the lasso catching her firmly and then Billy, Billy isn't there anymore.

36.

MATT HAS THE ROPE IN HIS HANDS AND HE
rolls his body on the ground, the rope winding round himself.
I dive to him and clutch him and we roll together, making of
ourselves a kind of reel, making sure that we have Veronica
anchored, firm. We spin and feel the weight of her, and she is
screaming, and we know the ledge is gone.

It takes maybe five minutes, that seem a lot longer, for
Mr. Koski to get the other end of that rope tied to his bumper, get wood under the wheels of the truck, get himself into

it, get jammed in reverse and us plowed back through the field and Veronica up over the ridge. And the three of us, just huffing, exhausted, humped in the dirt and furred with it, like small buffalo.

37.

BILLY LOOKS ODD WHEN THEY BRING HIM up from the bottom of the ridge. Have him up by first light in a litter strapped to the side of a white horse with spots of purple spilled like paint over its rump and down one leg. Mr. Fields and the sheriff's horse and rescue team do it. Billy looks like a drawing a kid would make, a stick figure with one arm going the wrong way and a collar bone snapped upward like one of those chicken bones you wish on, that bone pushing the skin up like a tent pole. Other than that he is okay.

He even manages to smile with blue, shivery lips when I tell him that other than the fact he is rearranged some, he looks fine. And when he gives me a grin in that half-smiling way of his, I know he really is all right and that things are all right between him and me. Then they slide him into Mr. Anapolini's ambulance, slick as a pizza into an oven, and he is off to the mercy of cute nurses and ice cream, fresh sheets, and no sleeping with Georgie in his bed for a time.

None of us tell how we'd thought those two had maybe gone up there to fly away, forever, even though they hadn't. I believed Veronica when she said they just went there to be alone. She was too scared to lie. But we all stick to the story I gave anyway—that we just went up there to get Veronica to take care of her little brother. Mr. Koski looks a little vague-minded, eyes smoked and hair curled with wind, when he tells that's why he'd brought us. Sooner or later they'll figure out we aren't telling the whole of what we'd known or thought, but for now no one is pressing us.

There are horse trailers up there, and Mr. and Mrs. Cheng and my grandpa Leonardo talking to the authorities about us for the second time in a couple of months, which I know isn't going to go over big with my dad when he shows up in a day or two. I already know I should go ahead and sign my life away to Monsignor and all the chores he can dream up for me round the church. His favorite is making a fellow scrape old paint from the wooden basement window frames, and I know I'll be living underground, guilty as Hitler, for a while. I hope someone remembers we saved those two. But I know my folks already think I have too much of a knack for finding trouble, and they won't care if it is trouble I am getting into or trouble I am getting somebody else out of.

Even Miss Farisi shows up that morning on the ridge. Comes in Mr. Edmund's new Chevy. She's got on her lion tamer outfit, though it's as mussed as her hair, and she doesn't say a thing, just hugs us, first with her eyes and then stooping down to clutch Georgie and then over to Veronica, who sobs into her shoulder all shuddery and released.

And then she hugs me, and I let that hug go all the way into me. She hugs Sammy and Luke and Matt and Mark, too. All hugged, proper and true. And they line right up for her hugging and don't act too big for it at all. That night had taken any phony pride we'd had, took it all, as it should.

38.

BILLY GOT A BIG PLASTER CAST IN A SLING
and a shoulder and neck brace contraption that was so
cool that Alice-Ann and Aurora made sketches in case they
decided to try making one for Alfred, and Billy had to promise
he'd save the thing for Georgie once he was mended. Three
days later, when he came home, we all signed every inch of
it except one spot he never said, but we knew, was saved
for Veronica. Once everybody calmed down a bit, I knew we
could tell it all to Grandpa, tell how we were making our

America same as his generation had, and he'd understand.

Once Billy was home, I did tell, and he and my mom moved Edgar and Jeffers into our bedrooms till Mrs. Jensen found them an apartment. Those two slept in my bed, but I guess I owed it to them for thinking the worst of them all that time that I did. They'd been mad, but hadn't really done anything except not like us and follow us some. Mrs. Jensen slept in the twin's room, and they slept in Margarita's. Margarita slept with Shawna, and Georgie slept on the floor and Rufus slept with him and somehow knew to take care and not roll over and crush him. I slept in Uncle Charlie's room and he slept in his chair out on the porch, which saved him his one chore of going up to bed every night. My dad came home to get some rest and listened some, but mostly he slept and didn't ask much. And so then it seemed that the whole house slept, with a soft sighing the wind made coming and going in and out of the screened windows we usually left open well into fall. Even the little flowers my mother grew and placed in the windowsills seemed to sleep, closing each night like eyes that had seen enough for a while and needed deep resting. And Alfred the cat slept, and probably the mice he dreamt of slept too, because all was relaxed then, and even my name, Paolo, was a blessing that dozed on my lips as I drifted off every night.

Maybe then, and certainly later, lots in Orange Grove, and I heard in Reedley, too, made some gossip out of the fact those two were of different races. That was when Billy was well enough for them to go round Orange Grove holding hands, because Mrs. Cheng and my mom got together and decided it, and then took Matthew and me along and talked Mr. Cheng into allowing it. But all of us who'd been there that morning knew then, and ever after, that we were the same, all of us. All of us could care about somebody enough to risk our very lives, could be that scared of losing them. There's no profit in trying to leave anyone out and no truth in it either. There's always going to be some that don't see it that way, but why should they be the ones who tell the rest how to live?

I wonder will I always remember that morning up on the ridge with the blue and pink sky swelling out like an atomic bomb in slow motion over the valley, we still standing around drinking hot chocolate and wearing Mrs. Cheng's blankets round our shoulders like Plains Indians and Georgie saying, "Paolo?" Just saying my name and looking into my eyes, I think, for me to give him some answer I didn't have. Talking out of nerves, I suppose.

I remember just putting my hand on his shoulder.

And he says, "Paolo, I think I could paint that sky and maybe me and you, too, put us standing in front of it. Miss Farisi could help me. Maybe do it with crayons."

I look down into his face, opened up, a big sunflower, trusting. "Think we could sell it for a dollar ninety-five?"

"I don't know, why?"

"Forget about it," I say, and then, "Yeah, you can color us here. It's a good place."

"I know," Georgie says, thoughtful.

"You know," I add, "if you're going to put us in your picture, then you should put everybody in, along with the sky."

"Everybody?"

"Yeah," I say, looking out at the distance. "Color us all."

"Okay," he says.

"Okay," I say.

"Hey, look, Paolo," he says, sudden, and I think he means watch Mr. Fields acting gentle as a man could, petting his horse and whispering to it like a girl and that horse not looking cross-eyed at all because, once again, you don't know who a person is till you see for yourself how they really are. But he's not pointing at that, he's pointing up, higher, way up in the sky, and I think he is pointing out the last morning stars that are fading, stars that will always remind me some of little winking candles of lanterns floating out, but he's not.

"Look," he says, his arm straight up. And I throw back my

head and see it, a hawk, a red-tailed one, tracing a circle of curiosity over us, swinging slow, round and round, counterclockwise and rising. "See," he says, smiling, little-kid sure, "the world's turning, just the way it's supposed to."

And I see that my brother is right. It is.